S
SNEDECKER.

S
c.1   Snedecker

AUTHOR

Forgotten Daughter

TITLE

DATE LOANED	BORROWER'S NAME	DATE RETURNED
	Eleanor M.	306
SEP. 21 1982	Martha Suarez	307
SEP 28 1982	uadalupe a.	314
April 11 1983	Rebecca Barabutis	314
	Raquel Loera	313
	Laura Fens	313
	KaedA MARou	305

© THE BAKER & TAYLOR CO.

THE FORGOTTEN DAUGHTER

Books by Caroline Dale Snedeker

THE PERILOUS SEAT

THE SPARTAN

THERAS AND HIS TOWN

DOWNRIGHT DENCEY

THE BECKONING ROAD

THE BLACK ARROWHEAD

THE TOWN OF THE FEARLESS

THE FORGOTTEN DAUGHTER

UNCHARTED WAYS

THE WHITE ISLE

LUKE'S QUEST

THE FORGOTTEN DAUGHTER

Caroline Dale Snedeker

DOUBLEDAY & COMPANY, INC.   GARDEN CITY, NEW YORK

CONTENTS

CONTENTS

To my young cousin
and dear friend
Elizabeth Waite Crawford
who lives in our home
on the gulf

CHAPTER 1

The Mountains of Samnium

Beauty lies upon the land like a visible light, for the land is Italy. But it is an Italy we seldom see —a place of northern aspect. Monstrous mountain-sides heave upward, clothed with fir forests, upward to where the bare cliffs soar against the sky. The valleys are narrow clefts, purple or black in their depth. In the wider vales sheep paths go winding along the hillsides, tiny parallel paths too narrow for human foot, cut deep by the knife-like hoofs of goat and ewe. They are the only sign of human habitation. In later centuries these hills will be crowned with monastery, abbey, castle, and the lower hill with its town, like a nest of turrets within the circling wall, giving the whole scene a meaning, an aspect of thought, of human effort and romance. But now the vista is utterly alone, menacing. The mountains are withdrawn into themselves and have no commerce with the littleness of man.

The air comes sharply chill, breathing that almost arctic fragrance of fir trees basked in the sun. Yet strangely over this northern coldness arches the brilliance of an Italian sky.

"Oh, our sky—but that is always bright," say the loving Latins.

So now in this ancient Samnium the fir forests take on purples unbelievable, the high cliffs are glorified with golden light, and the far distances melt into amethyst and violet, like dream places of the gods. Light is light and is in itself almost a divinity.

Halfway up a wooded mountain, a hut leaned against a cliff, viewing to the full this passionate loveliness. It was, even for that ancient day when it stood there, a hut of antique form. Woven of wattles and daubed with mud, roofed with the same—such huts the earliest inhabitants of Europe had made for themselves before the Romans came, and even now in remote places far from Rome this manner of building lingered.

Inside the hut all the hill beauty was quenched like a candle—windowless, dim, and the space of it almost filled with two upright looms. It was close, smelling of sheep wool piled high in baskets, and of the heated bodies of the workers. A woman and a child we would call them, but to the Romans they were two women. The younger, twelve years old, was of the marriageable age in Roman law.

The older woman worked steadily, pacing, pacing before her loom. She might be called beautiful, with her faint reminder of the grave reliefs on the Sacred Way at Athens. But she was no rounded, well-fed matron, but thin, aged before her time and stooped as weavers grow to be. The child worked with en-

ergy and swiftness, now bending as she threw the
shuttle through the warp, now darting as she caught
it on the other side and threw it back again, now
stooping as she lifted the level rod which held the
thread ends in groups for the pattern, jerking each
rod forward in its turn. So she darted like a dragon
fly, and was like a dragon fly for thinness and wary
impatience.

For this industry these two received no pay. They
were slaves.

The older woman watched the younger anxiously.
Presently she spoke. Her speech was Greek—not
Attic but Æolic Greek, a more archaic form.

"Chloé, my darling, you have knotted the thread.
See there and there. And the fabric is all uneven.
It must not be tight and loose by turns."

The child did not answer, only weaving faster as
though to outdistance reproof.

"You know what Davus will do if the fabric is
poor. My dear, it must be ripped out. Wait, wait!"

The woman stopped her work. The child also
stopped, dropping her shuttle to the ground.

"No, no! Melissa, please do not unweave it. It is
so near done, please do not unweave it. If I finish
I can go out a little while and play." Tears and
rebellion were in her voice; but she stood aside
while Melissa began patiently to throw the shuttle
back through the old paths, taking out the thread.
With every throw Chloé's breath drew quick in sobbing protest.

"There, dear heart," said Melissa at last. "More should really come out, but perhaps Davus will not notice. Oh, he must not be angry! Not again with you—you know what he will do."

She did not touch Chloé, nor caress her. It was as if she feared to break the child's control. Only the look which brushed past the little figure taking its place again in front of the loom was one of infinite brooding and love.

And now again the soft sounds of weaving filled the room. But from working swiftly Chloé now worked slowly and more slowly—hands trembling with suppressed reluctance, the work, also, not much better than before. Slower, almost stopping at times, like a clock running down.

"Try, do try!" Melissa warned her almost in a whisper. "Oh," (with sudden passion) "I cannot stand it if he whips you again!"

Chloé did try. She worked a little better for a while. Then the clock slowed again. Her hands trembled and her breath fluttered. She spoke to herself:

"I haven't been out by the stream for days, and days, and *days*. The sun gets up before the night is done; and then we begin, and it's never, never, never until he sets. Apollo doesn't care. I prayed to him to make the days shorter."

"My dear," interposed Melissa, "the days are growing longer with the spring. Even Apollo cannot help that."

"If he cannot help it, then he is no god. But he does not care. He does not care."

The grief of this seemed to mingle with the grief of the weaving. The young awakening mind had thought it out and thought it to despair. Centuries of keenness and originality lay behind this child— the life of far-away islands in the Ægean Sea. Even her common words betrayed this. The beauty of the old speech of Sappho and Alkæus was in every sentence. As for herself she was small and angular; and her black hair, which was never tended nor brushed, hung in elf locks about her face.

Again silence in the hut, the silence of weaving. Outside, the sunshine pulsated among the hills, distances smiled with infinite meaning, purity and breathful air were rife. Inside, the dimness and half-light, the closeness like the very smell of sorrow.

Presently the child's thread knotted, she unfastened it, but another tangled with it, a third, a whole group, possessed as it were with evil. With a gasp she threw down the shuttle and covered her face with her hands.

Melissa knew these signs. She knew there was no use to urge the exhausted fingers. There was no more work in them. She moved to the child and patted her softly.

"Stand here," she said, "as if you were working. There, hold the shuttle so if Davus comes he cannot tell. Shall I sing?"

Chloé nodded.

"Shall I sing the sleep song which Leto sang to her little ones on Delos Isle; or perhaps of Orpheus when his beloved lyre washed ashore on Lesbos and gave us forever the gift of song?"

"No, no!" said Chloé hastily. "Sing the one about you and me and about our home in Lesbos. Sing it! So we can forget, make the hut disappear."

And with sweet patience Melissa began. Sometimes she chanted in slow, monotonous measures. Sometimes she talked in a straightforward narrative of events. Both of them knew the tale by heart. Melissa's telling had fallen into a set, unaltered form. That mattered not. For these two there were no books or the knowledge to read them. So the sweet source of song was open to them. That source from which all great books are taken, but from which no book is able to gather all the living sweetness. Melissa's song was rude and simple, but it had that power.

CHAPTER 2

Melissa Sings

Elpenor beginneth the tale. Elpenor whose life was of the sea. He it was who became our undoing, though all unwitting. A man of keen wit, beautiful to look upon was he, tall and swift of foot. All the songs of Lesbos were known to him: Sappho, Alkæus, and all the Little Iliad. And those yet older songs which only the shepherds know, or the sailors at work upon the fast-going ship. These songs beat with rhythm as though the stamping of feet were in them. All these he sang to his lyre, sitting by the salt sea when the sun went down and all the ways were darkened.

"We folk of Eresus (for Eresus was our own town in Lesbos) would come forth from our houses to listen. His voice was sweet beyond all telling. It was for this that we loved his homecoming. Seldom was he with us, for his life was of the sea.

"Elpenor was thy kinsman, Chloé, of thy same blood. His gods were thine. Very different was he from his brother Anaxion, him that was thy dear mother's father, and who might indeed be called the father of our town, for to him came all the folk of Eresus for judgment in their quarreling. And whatever thing he judged, by that they abode, for wise and just was he, and in him was no guile. Anaxion was ever with us, nor left he even for a day the violet, shining Lesbos, being happy to increase his flocks and the vines which greened the warm hills.

"But Elpenor went ever afar. A noble ship was his, and he the captain thereof. Oft he journeyed to Lemnos and brought thence the clay earth that will cure all manner of disease. Again he went southward carrying oil and Lesbian wine.

"'And even as on the plain a yoke of four stallions comes springing all together beneath the lash, leaping high and speedily accomplishing the way, so leaped the bow of that ship, and the dark wave of the sounding sea rushed mightily in the wake, and she ran ever surely on her way, nor could a circling hawk keep pace with her—of wingèd things the swiftest. Even thus she lightly sped and cleft the waves of the sea.'"

As Melissa sang of the ship, the rhythm of her song changed with an overpowering mastery. Chloé lifted her head and began to hum with her. Neither Chloé, who listened, nor Melissa, who sang, knew that the ship song was of Homer. They only knew it was their own, something heard from earliest childhood, sung by their fathers, aye, by the gods themselves.

After the ship song Melissa did not return to her

former rhythm but swept along in sounding hexameters.

"The ship flew southward and came to the isle of Tenos, there where lie the sons of Æolus in their graves, slain by Heracles. Then sped they to the isle of Delos."

"And there was born Apollo the son of Leto, the dear son of Light," chimed in Chloé. She turned away from her loom toward Melissa, but Melissa did not dare to reprove her, being glad for the brightness that was growing in her face.

"Then sailed he to Crete, the isle of peaked hills. From Crete he sailed southward and eastward over a vast sea even to Egypt, for the gods had accepted his gifts and gave him fair winds ever. There sold he all his cargo at a great price, and with much gold he set sail for home.

"But now the Shaker-of-the-Earth, lord of the sounding sea, was turned against Elpenor. Great winds he sent, out of the east and south, which drave the ship and tore the sail in shreds. For days they labored, but the ship was beyond the help of mortal man; and on the third day they went ashore upon Crete, where the ship was lost and all the men save one with Elpenor.

"Now that ship and the cargo thereof were all that he owned on earth. He became a beggar, and as a beggar he wandered in Crete, unable to win home. There he met with desperate Cretan men who took him into their ship and made him their captain, for that he was shrewd in the ways of the sea. In that ship they raided the shore of Lacedæmon and the ports of the Cyclades. They became sea thieves, 'sea swallows' we call them, they that fly upon the sea and rob the ports of men.

"But certain Romans stationed at Rhodes heard of that raiding and by command of their general were sent forth, soldiers in a ship to catch Elpenor, kill him, and sink the ship. Lævinus it was who commanded the Romans on that errand."

At the word "Lævinus" Chloé caught her breath.

"Lævinus, my father," she whispered, and a hatred stared out of her eyes and made them wide and alarmed.

"Yea, thy father or thine owner," echoed Melissa, hating also. "But at this time he was not thy father, but a youth slim and quick-footed, having as it were the first down upon his lip. Strange it was that one so young should be a centurion in the army.

"Now the Romans who rob under their law are not willing that anyone should rob without the law. And they had made them a great oath that no man should harry the coasts of our Ægean Sea. Ahai—that sea that once was all our own with islands-of-freedom in it.

"Then late one night, when all in Eresus-town were sleeping, came Elpenor home in a shallop, and gat him to Anaxion's house and begged him to save him. Anaxion, though he knew the danger of such harboring, was fain to help his brother. So he put him in a cave of the hills that are back of the town.

No one in the house knew of this, not his daughter
Chloé (thy mother to be), not his sons, not his lady
wife, for she was not then living, nor any slave in the
house.

"Only I and my father knew. Because my father
was exegete and priest of the temple and Anaxion's
dearest friend. But I it was who took Elpenor's food
to him. In the deep midnight I took it, laboring up
the hillside in the rain—or it might be under a moon-
less sky, glad of heart to bring him food and wine.
But on moonlit nights when our isle is steeped in
light, and all the headlands afar dream in divine
beauty, then must I bide at home. Then Elpenor sat
hungry in his cave. I begged him to sit so within the
cave, nor come forth nor be seen of any. But Elpenor
was careless—yea, of himself and of others. There
were Romans in Mytilene who came down to hunt
the boar in the Ortymnus Mountains. Perhaps they
saw him and told. We do not know. We shall never
know."

Even as she wove the story, Melissa wove the
threads upon the loom, pacing faster and ever faster
—unconscious of how she worked and only conscious
of the tale. For already had her soul flown to her
beautiful island, and there it abode. But now she had
emptied her shuttle of all its thread and must need
sit by her loom, take up her distaff, and spin more.
There she sat, twisting off the woolen thread with
incredible swiftness. But Chloé dropped her thread
altogether. Creeping toward Melissa like a fascinated

bird, she knelt at her knees, and her wide eyes met Melissa's.

"Now the vineyards," she whispered, "and the summertime and the gathering of the grapes."

CHAPTER 3

Melissa Sings of the Vineyards

Melissa began again:

"Yea, the summer was now come, and in early morning we left the house in town and gat us up to the lesser house among the hills. Both were the dear homes of Anaxion.

"The day rose bright; but far out upon the sea was a mist—the mist of Euros, so we knew that soon would be a storm. Therefore would we harvest the grapes before the storm. The slaves brought forth baskets and ladders to stand upon that we might not bruise the vines, and shears wherewith to cut the heavy bunches of purple grapes. So early did we come to the vineyards that the nightingales were still singing in the thickets. Coolness and wet dew were there, and behold, as we walked, the sparkle of the dew moved ever before us over the fresh grass. The vines stood row upon row on the sunny hill, and the grapes thereof filled the whole air with a fragrance sweeter than Maron's wine which he gave to Odyssos. So did we fall to work.

"Chloé, Anaxion's lovely daughter, came with us to watch the vintage, and I to be her companion.

But Anaxion stayed below talking with his plough-men in the fields."

One might hear now the younger Chloé breathing in the hut like a hunted deer.

"The first we knew was a bitter cry, faint in the valley below—three times repeated. We turned about, but already now the Roman soldiers filled all the path, their swords bare, glittering in their hands and wet with the terrible work already done.

"We cried out, we leaped among the vines, tearing the precious vines as we ran up the hill. We ran! We ran! But they were among us. We were in the midst of the battle. Not long, not long!—for vintners could not contend with their shears against armed men. My darling Chloé was at my side. Suddenly a soldier caught her as it were a sheep or a pig from the stye, and holding her under his strong, foul arm, went hurrying down the hill. Another man caught me and held me so under his left arm, flourishing his sword in my face. Shrieks and terror, shrieks and terror; yet all the while, I was conscious of the dear path down which he ran—my captor. The path, the little stones I knew so well so close to my down-hanging face. The last time. The last time I should see those dear paths of home. I shrieked and cried out; but Chloé made no sound. My darling Chloé! What now could save her from death, or life worse than death? Bitter, bitter it is to be led away captive and to be a slave upon the earth."

"Bitter, bitter," repeated the younger Chloé's lips, but her voice made no sound.

"Suddenly there was a new voice," went on Melissa, "very clear and commanding. The running ceased, and in a flash I was set down in the path, where I sank half fainting. Chloé too was set upright; but she stood like a pillar of the temple, aye, a ruined temple that hath no roof, and the pillar stands alone, white, erect, and still.

"Lævinus, the Roman centurion, stood fronting her, panting in his armor. Perhaps he noted her beauty, for it would indeed be a dead man who would not note it.

" 'Well,' he said, taunting, 'you do not cry out like the others.'

" 'What have you done with my father?' she demanded.

" 'He is dead as he deserves.'

" 'You have killed him!' She advanced a step toward him. There was actual menace in her. He, armed and strong, and she in her fluttering dress. He looked at her as if amused that so weak a creature should defy him. Only a moment. He turned, calling a command to his herald, who straightway blew the trumpet for the men to gather toward the ship.

"Then Lævinus commanded us in Greek, though hard to be understood: 'Go forward; go down to the shore.'

"I rose, but I could only stagger, and the soldier carried me. As for Chloé, she stepped back in horror when the soldier clutched her again. Lævinus spoke a sharp Latin word, and with cringing look the man desisted. Then Chloé, with Lævinus behind her as if driving her, walked down the path. Down, down we went; through the deserted town. For the folk had seen the ship in the harbor and had fled to the hills. Who of them was dead? Who, pierced to the heart, lay bleeding in the coppice? We did not know. We shall never know. Doth my father live? Did Elpenor escape through the deep glens—he whom I loved most of all? Doth he live? I know not, I know not, I shall never know."

Melissa dropped her distaff, covered her face with her hands and rocked to and fro. Little did she guess what harm she did, drawing up sorrow from old wells of sorrow for the child.

Little Chloé reached toward her, pulling Melissa's hands apart.

"Tell more, tell more," she pleaded. "Tell until *I* come into it."

And with that strange control which the true singer has in the midst of emotion, Melissa began again—like a low chant:

"We were in the ship. We were in the Roman ship. Long we crouched there on the deck, under guard, while the Romans on shore were bringing down sheep from the hills, and wine and oil from the town. Lævinus had to shout to them as one shouts to a pack of dogs to make them desist. Then the sailors pulled up anchor, unbrailed the leathern sails. Slowly, slowly we came about and began to move down the harbor. Then did the folk on the deck wail to the mighty gods as they saw their home fading away and the dear headlands going into the mist.

"But I was past tears, as was Chloé also. Lævinus hurried by us in that busy haste of a ship's embarking, but even so he saw Chloé.

"'You are not weeping?' Again he seemed taunting her.

"'Those who are dead cannot weep,' she answered him.

"A startled look crossed his face. Busy as he was, he fetched a rope and tied her feet. He knew she would leap into the sea at the first chance."

"I hate him I hate him, tying my mother's feet!" whispered the child; and again the death paleness crossed her and widened her eyes.

"In the harbor had been the harbor quiet—for deep is our 'Euripos' and sheltered between two mighty headlands.

"But the instant we came into the open sea we knew that the storm had broken. The sky was dark, the water perfectly black beneath us, and the ship began to pitch and toss terribly. The Roman soldiers were all sick. Lævinus strode hither and yon, urging them to their duties. They were not sailors, but land soldiers, and Lævinus their land centurion. But the sailors themselves also were Romans—no island-born would have gone forth in that storm. We know our sea too well.

"Now torrents of rain fell upon the deck—and thick mist was everywhere. Already our beloved

Lesbos was hidden. Alas, when the gods fashion troubles, they fashion many at once, as it were a potter whirling pots upon a wheel, pot after pot, to cast them down upon men. Night came, and all the ways were darkened. The four winds of heaven brake forth upon the sea. The ship labored like a dragon in the deep: first it mounted toward high heaven, then sank into the water. And behold, a black wall of water would rise to one side the slanting deck. So hours passed.

"Suddenly Lævinus was there again, staggering and falling, so difficult it was to go. He whipped out his sword; I thought he was making ready to kill us, but instead he cut the ropes from Chloé's feet.

"'If the ship founders, you shall have your chance with the rest,' he said coldly.

"The instant he was gone, Chloé began to crawl along the deck toward our suffering townspeople. She crawled, for no man could walk on that hurling surface. They were weeping, groaning, some fainting with sickness and despair.

"She began to comfort them. One she would stroke with her hand, another upbraid for lack of courage, saying, 'We are Lesbians—no man shall be our master. There is always a door of escape.'

"I could not hear the words, but the weeping ceased at her comfort, and the groaning ones sat up as if taking heart. There was a young shepherdess of our mountains. To her she said, 'Weep not, Pero. Thou hast not so dire a fate as I—who am to be mated with my father's murderer.'

"We had not noticed Lævinus, but he had returned and was standing just above us.

"'What did you say?' he demanded, for he could in no wise hear for the storm.

"She turned and repeated her words, clear and straightforward.

"'I did not kill your father,' he answered harshly. 'The men killed him in the field before I came.'

"Almost it was an excuse. But why should he excuse or explain? I saw her bow her head quickly to keep back the tears. But Lævinus had hurried away. He seemed everywhere at once, trying to quell the confusion, to keep hope in his soldiers, and to keep the sailors at work. Always with him was the captain of the ship, walking at his side.

"Chloé sat in a heap, quite still, quite still. It was long ere she lifted her head. Then she moved to where Kleus, our neighbor, a seaman, crouched near us. Immediately he spoke.

"'Lady, we are lost,' he told her. 'The captain has lost his way. We are headed straight for the rocks of Halonnesus.'

"'Ah! Then that is well,' she answered.

"'Not well for me, Chloé. I want to return to my home and my people.'

"'Do you know where we are?'

"'I know well enough to steer us off the rocks of Halonnesus. Twice before have I been caught in this wind. We seamen know it well. Aye, once I lost my ship.'

"He seized her arm and shook it.

"'It is you who must tell the centurion!' he cried. 'He would not listen to me, but he would to you.'

"'Oh, no, no, no! I cannot beg of him. I do not want him to listen. I want the ship to go down.'

"'Then you will kill us all.'

"For long she sat there heaped together; not sobbing, but shaking as if with a chill. Then she lifted her head. She had not long to wait. When Lævinus came near enough to see, she rose and staggered to him.

"She told what Kleus had said. Then again Lævinus hurried away; but soon he returned with the captain.

"'This captain confesses at last,' he said angrily, 'he is ignorant where we are. This seaman here—do you know him?'

"'Aye, I know him,' she answered, 'and he knows the sea. In Eresus we trust him.' Then she came back and fell upon the deck beside me. She looked as though her heart were breaking.

"But Lævinus took Kleus away and put him in command of the ship.

"Ah, how can I recall that night? The storm increased. The wind cried about our ears like a power gone mad. The bolts of Zeus fell from the sky, and his voice thundered. The great mast of the ship snapped and came hurtling down upon the deck, and the sail smothered us all. Oh, what a shrieking went up then! We struggled from under the sail, all helping one another. The sailors ran every way, chopping the ropes to free the sail from the mast.

"Suddenly Lævinus lifted the last of the leather sail off us and fell on his knees beside Chloé and gathered her in his arms.

"'Are you alive, alive, alive?' he cried out wildly. 'Where did it hit you? Oh, are you whole and alive?'

"We were so near death then that even I did not think it strange for Lævinus to do this; and Chloé sank into his arms as if their warmth protected her. He took her hands, warming them against his lips, his throat.

"'Great gods, how I love you!' he said softly under his breath. 'Great gods, how I love you!' He seemed in an amazement.

"Another scream went up from the after deck, and Lævinus scrambled to his feet and ran off to quell it. I never knew what it was. For he came straightway back, dragging a part of the mast, and tied Chloé to it. She was dumb as a sheep at shearing. Then he dragged up a lesser piece and strapped me to it.

"'Pray to the gods, mother, pray to the gods,' he said and was again gone.

"Never shall I forget that long, long night. Nor how the grey day broke slowly and late over the sea. Not like light, but another kind of darkness. The ship was beyond any man's guidance then. All day the storm raged. But toward nightfall the wind slowly, slowly abated. We slept that night wrapped in a piece of sail. We were too fordone to keep awake, though we tried. The next morning the clouds broke; though the wind still raged—no ordinary storm. We were far north now.

"And on the third day Kleus, as by some god-given seeing, guided the ship into the Gulf of Toronaicus —into a sheltered bay that he knew."

CHAPTER 4

Melissa Sings of the Villa

Oh, the beautifulness of haven after the anger of the sea! The quiet firmness of earth after Poseidon's wrath! We poured forth from the ship as bees in a swarm out of their dark hive. Some kissed the pebbly beach. Others stood in a daze. Above the bank of the shore was a meadow; and sweeter than the wild rose came the smell of grass in the sun.

" 'Search for a spring,' cried the people. For the first need of those rescued from the sea is pure water to drink from the nymphs and Mother Ge.

"Chloé and I stood together on the shore, timid and moveless, when Lævinus approached us.

" 'Come with me,' he said to Chloé. 'We too will search for a spring.'

"She cowered back toward me.

" 'Are you afraid of nothing in the world—me excepted?' he asked. 'There is no girl in all Rome who would act as you acted, those days of storm, encouraging your people. It was you who saved the ship. For this I love you.'

" 'Kleus saved the ship,' she said earnestly. She hoped he would free Kleus and send him home.

" 'Modesty becometh a woman,' he answered, and

then was lost gazing into her eyes. His whole being seemed to grow tender and kind, as though he were no longer a Roman but a friend. Her head bowed before his gaze, and I saw her hands tremble.

"'You have no need to fear me,' he spoke again. 'You will never have need to fear. I shall marry you when we come to Rome. It is you and none other I will have for my wife.'

"She looked up, astonished. She had expected all her life long to be a slave."

"And she was, she was, she was," cried out the child in the hut, beating her hands together as though it were she suffering instead of her mother.

"Then," went on Melissa, "he put out his hand once more."

"'Come,' he said, 'let us search for the spring.'

"Impulsively she put her hand in his. Together they clambered up the bank. A few moments later they were running hand in hand toward those others who searched for the spring.

"It was a long, long voyage to Rome. Kleus guided the ship down the Ægean past the dear, dear isles, past Malea. We hoped Lævinus would free him for this. But he did not free him. After that the Romans sailed us onward to Rome. There did Lævinus get dismissal from his company. And there he married Chloé—not by that most solemn marriage before their pontifex in the Forum, but by that other marriage which is allowed between a Roman and a Greek. He did not take Chloé to his home. He told

that his father was in Spain governing a city, and the
lady mother with him; perhaps that was so.

"Then in a cart we rode out of the city Rome, the
slaves walking, and we journeyed to the hills, hither
to this far-off villa. It was a farmstead then—our
Villa Caracinia—one tall narrow house within a high
wall, the slave sheds huddled close, and the cattle
all about it and the sheep bleating in their folds. A
rude place and unclean. But Lævinus at once began
to better it. He let pull down the sheds, and built
slave quarters to one side downward on the hill. He
made the *olivaria* for oil, and the *vinaria* with the
great wine press therein—thou hast seen them—and
many folds for sheep.

"He enlarged the atrium of the house and brought
thereto the pure water from the hills in a fountain.
The cattle place he made a garden wherein he
planted the flowers that Chloé loved, violets and
roses for garlands like those in Lesbos. In that garden
he builded a portico of marble where Chloé might
sit and spin and where they took their meals. Chloé
was indeed his wife. Not as the Greek wife who must
stay in her own quarters above the stairs; but the
Roman wife who is free of all the house, who meets
his friends in the atrium—those few friends who
would come to so remote a place. Chloé was *matrona,*
and all the slaves obeyed her. In those days there
was a shining in her face.

"It was I who waited upon the table, and oft when
Chloé had given greeting and retired to her own
place, I would hear Lævinus talking of her to his

guest. 'Is she not beautiful, and her dignity rare and flowerlike? Chloé is her name, and Chloé her nature, too.' Then, rising up from his couch for very eagerness, he would tell always that same tale of the storm and the ship, how she encouraged her people and feared not death; but found for him and for all of us a way of escape from the sea. He had not only love for her but pride in her. So it seemed! So it seemed!

"Sometimes he journeyed to Rome or Neapolis to buy a better ram, or ewes, sometimes to buy men—the strong Iberian slaves or Gauls from the north to tend the sheep. For he purposed to make our Villa Caracinia a great enterprise.

"'My father,' he said, 'will be glad when he returns to Rome to see how I have mended our fortune.' And in that he seemed joyous. Then he said also, 'I will make this place a place of spinning; the wool that we get from the sheep shall be made into garments, and therefrom I will get much gold.'

"Thus he made the place larger. He would rise at dawn to go forth upon the hills. He had no *vilicus* in those days; but viewed the work himself. We wondered at this, Chloé and I, for no Greek would leave his city to live among the hills. But with the Romans it is otherwise. Farming is a pride to them—equal, almost, to their pride in Rome.

"At the end of the first year was born their son, thy brother. If he had lived, perhaps all would have been otherwise. For a son lifteth up a house, but a daughter not so. For three months stayed he with us,

a buxom child, and then he died. That was their
first sorrow. Then all Chloé's hope, her daily sacrifice
at the altar, was for another son.

"But Lævinus never lifted from that sorrow. He
grew morose and strange, harsh with the slaves and
drove them ever harder at the work. 'It had been
better,' he said, 'if our son had lived.' As though the
blame were hers. There seemed on him a cloud by
day and night, as though a cloud of shame."

The child Chloé in the hut stirred on her knees as
though in fear of what was coming.

"Then one day he must away to Rome to take the
wool and woven garments to the market. It was a
goodly yield. He seemed happy in that going, suddenly light-hearted as if glad to go. He kissed Chloé
as he always did and said to her:

"'All will be well. Have no fear. I have determined. All will be well.'

"We knew not what he meant. But whatever he
meant it was deception. He left Bion the Bœotian in
charge of the farm work. He was gone.

"The time allotted passed and still he came not
again. The summer was very hot. Chloé feared he
had died of the heat in Rome. For always he had
sent her some word by a slave; but no word came.
The moon that had been a sickle in the sky came
to the full and waned again. And, alas, my Chloé
waned with it. Pale and fordone was she. She could
scarce walk to the altar when she brought her sacrifice to pray for his sake. And still she trusted him.
But the slaves who had before had respect for her

began to treat her coldly. Their faces sneered when they served her. We heard no word from Rome—no word at all.

"Then suddenly one eventide came Davus, the new slave foreman. Into the atrium he walked with his men as though he were indeed the owner. He summoned Chloé. But before he called, she came hurrying from her room.

"'Is Lævinus well? Tell me he is alive and well!'

"He answered impatiently before she had finished:

"'Well? Of course he is well. But Lævinus will not return. He sends me to tell you he is married to Helvia in Rome. Also he has sailed to Egypt with his century.'

"Chloé fell to the floor as though he had struck her. I gathered her up in my arms as best I might and carried her quickly away. All that night we sat in her room, not speaking to each other. Darkness had closed upon our minds; and we knew not whither to grope our way.

"So passed three days. I feared Davus. I greatly feared him. There was strange purpose in his face when he looked at us. Purpose and doubt. At night I would hear him stealing past our door. Yet he came not in. But I believed that he had orders to kill Chloé or perhaps to sell her far away—orders which somehow he dared not fulfill. I know not! I know not!

"But one morning he came to our room. His mind was made up.

"'I have found a place—a hut in the hillside. Ye shall go——'"

CHAPTER 5

The Cruel Vilicus

Suddenly the door of the slave hut darkened.
Davus himself stood here. Davus the vilicus staring
into the darkness.

"Ahai," he laughed gruffly, "what do I see? Two
ladies singing in their atrium—two ladies, by Pollux!"

Chloé gave a sharp cry and hid behind Melissa.

"How many times have I told you not to gossip
and play? What's a slave for?"

Melissa obediently rose and staggered to him.
"Don't whip the little one. It was I that talked.
Don't whip the little one," she was crying.

He grasped her arm roughly and pulled her outside where he could better wield the whip. There he
whipped her. Chloé, half dying in the hut, could
hear the lashes. Melissa uttered no cries. The lashes
stopped. He was done with Melissa.

Again the door darkened. Now, *now* he seized herself, Chloé. Chloé lost consciousness—or was she supremely conscious? For, all her life afterward, in her
dreams, she was to feel that clutch, and re-live that
moment. He dragged her outside into the beautiful
place God had made. He began!

It was not his largest whip with the thongs—the one he used for beating the shepherds; but it was bad enough—bad enough; made of leather and long. It twisted like a serpent when it fell. Chloé kept her hands over her eyes to save them. Every slave did that.

Lash, lash, lash! The whistle of the whip sounded in the air, and with every blow the child seemed to shrink smaller upon the earth.

At last it ceased. The whip, the whistling, the blows—ceased. She heard the steps of Davus and his men going down the path. She lay where they left her. Melissa seemed to be speaking to her; but it was as though she did not hear. She began to creep on hands and knees like a hurt animal. She crept under the bushes, and there she stayed.

When Melissa tried to pull her out, she resisted so fiercely that it seemed best to let her lie there. Melissa crouched by the door of the hut, dazed and aching. All was unreal like dreaming. About midnight it began to rain. Again Melissa went to the bushes. She stooped and pulled at the little hand.

"If she is sleeping I will not wake her," she thought, "even though it rains."

But this time the child's hand gave to her touch. Melissa pulled again softly.

"My darling come, come," she whispered.

Suddenly Chloé pushed back the bushes—sat up. She threw both arms about Melissa.

"Melissa, I love you, I love you, I love you," she cried before the storm of tears overtook her.

Melissa almost carried her into the hut. There she sat down, drew Chloé to her lap and held her close. Thus would she keep them both warmer.

All night long she remained until Chloé relaxed into sleep; and Melissa still sat wide-eyed above her. So might Demeter have sat with her child Persephone in her arms—the pietà of the Grecian world —grieving that her daughter must dwell in the darkness of Hades and the blackness of the departed.

So sorrow, wide as the mountains, dwelt in the contracted hut. And love contended with it for mastery.

Slavery was like this. We say we have slavery today in factory and machine shop—but slavery was different—slavery was like this.

CHAPTER 6

The Deserted Villa

In the hillside hut Chloé, the daughter of Lævinus, had been born; and Chloé, the Lesbian, had died. She had been buried beside the hut on the hill, the grave, not a mound but a sunken place into which Melissa placed rough stones to keep it from disappearing ever entirely.

A few days after her death, a boy appeared hastily, secretly, from the villa, breathless with running.

"Hurry, Melissa," he panted. "Hide the baby. A brother of Lævinus is come. He is asking about Chloé. When they told him she is dead, he said, 'I must be sure. Where did you bury her?' Davus is bringing him up the hill."

Melissa could only guess what it meant. Surely to do more harm. She caught up the baby and ran with it into the forest. There she hid in a deep glen until nightfall. Then came the boy again with glad face.

"They have gone. They stood and looked at the grave. The Roman shook his head; and then they searched the hut. They could not find you and so went away."

Melissa stayed with the baby in the wood until she heard the Roman had gone home again. So the little Chloé began her life in the almost secret hut.

After this hasty visit of Lævinus's brother, the Roman owners did not once come to the farm. They seemed to avoid the place, or in any case regarded it merely as a business enterprise, from which the returns, reported regularly by the vilicus, were satisfactory. Such absentee-owned farms were becoming more and more common in Italy at this time. The simple Roman farmer—backbone of the republic— was sadly crowded out.

So the farm at Villa Caracinia went on from day to day—from year to year, and life in the hut was unchanged. Davus whipped the child often. But even his stupidity had to see at last that it did no good. Little Chloé's work was bungled and poor, and grew less in bulk rather than more for his whippings. He did not want her to die. That might be dangerous. Was she not after all the child of his younger master? Lævinus did not care for her now, but if he ever did, might not Davus receive a reward? It was Davus's own plan anyway, saving her in the first place. It was worth the gamble.

As for little Chloé, she neither lived nor died. She awoke in the morning. She sat at the loom. She untangled the threads. She ate the rough cakes Melissa gave her, the half-spoiled olives and slave wine, scarcely knowing that the feeling she had after it was unsatisfied hunger. There was one meal a day. It did not occur to her that there should be more.

Sometimes on holidays Melissa would take her down to the villa. It was scarcely a pleasure. It seemed to fan alive her hatred of her father—the resentment that smoldered in her all her days. Yes, there was the great olive press which Lævinus had caused to be placed there—the slaves working and sweating as they pressed out the oil. There the vinaria where they made the wine to be sent to Rome, for him to drink.

In the great vaulted kitchen, there were always a number of slaves hanging about; and Robina, the cook, busy and contented. Melissa held herself better than the slaves; but Robina was irresistible. She was fat and well liking—ruler of her domain. On cold evenings, when the slaves gathered like flies toward the kitchen warmth, Robina would drive them forth with her fists and raucous cries. Or if she was in a good mood, which meant if she had some news to tell, she would welcome them in, regale them with her stories and with bits from the table which she always managed to have at hand.

More rarely she was in a listening mood and would let them gossip and laugh by the fire. For Melissa, however, she had a peculiar liking, partly because Melissa really never sought entrance to the kitchen, and because about Melissa still lingered a little honor of the former time.

One autumn day when Melissa and Chloé had come down to quarters for more wool, Robina fairly dragged them over the threshold.

"Come in, come in out of the rain. Isn't it the

cruelty of Jupiter to send a rain on a holiday! And me—I was going to Aufidena for the festival. The others went. Byrsa cried till I let her go. Not me. Where's the fun if you're wet to the skin? There, sit by the fire, little one." She pushed Chloé toward the great open fireplace, where an iron pot with feet stood steaming among the glowing fagots.

"She don't get no fatter, does she?" she said to Melissa.

"No," answered Melissa sadly. "Work and poor food are neither of them fattening."

"Ahai, and she don't get no prettier neither." Robina always talked before Chloé as though she were totally deaf. "Strange, she don't look a thing like her mother. *She* was pretty. No wonder Lævinus was crazy about her. Do you think the little one's like *him,* maybe?"

"Oh, no, no, no!" put in Chloé. She was afraid of Robina with her robust ways.

"I'm sure not," hastened Melissa.

Robina with head to one side regarded Chloé. "I don't know now. The nose—that's certainly like his."

Chloé clapped her hand over her nose as if to hide it from the world.

Melissa changed the subject.

"Hasn't the rain hurt the olives? I was afraid it would."

"Afraid! I'm glad. The first crop was enough for the oil. And now all the second's blown to the ground. The boys picked 'em up. I've got a lot for myself." A sudden thought struck Robina. "Say, now

—has the little one here ever seen her mother's room in the house?"

"Of course not," asserted Melissa. "We would not go into Davus's quarters."

"Davus! Those rooms don't belong to him. He wouldn't dare. He lives where he should by the front gate, and his wife, too. He's gone now to Rome to sell the weaving and make report to the master. Why don't you take her in where her mother used to be?"

To Chloé it was as if a fountain had suddenly bubbled up from a hidden source—this wish to see where her mother had lived—this wish so impossible that she had not even wished it before. She sprang up from the hearth.

"Please, Melissa—let me see it. Take me to see it."

"Are you sure——" Melissa hesitated. "Sure that Davus is gone?"

"Sure as omens," declared Robina. "Didn't I see him go? Hurry along, now. When you come back I'll give ye both some soup."

Melissa doubtfully took Chloé's hand. She still acted toward Chloé as though she were a little child. Perhaps because she was so small for her age—so hesitating and timid. She led her through the echoing kitchen into the triclinium, where stood the dining table, bare of dishes or cloth; into an open corridor and thence to a cell-like room.

"This was her room," said her voice of awe. "There

was another larger room for her and Lævinus, but
this was her very own."

It was one of those small, dim cellas which the
Romans always used for sleeping, lighted only from
the inner court. It contained a narrow bed, a small
table on which was a metal mirror, a chest for
clothes, and a chair on which lay a distaff full of
wool as though the departed one had but just laid
it down.

Who can account for the hidden places of reverence that lie in a child's mind? This room once
habited by the Lesbian Chloé was such a place to
Chloé the slave. Not because the elder Chloé had
been her mother (though that perhaps gave it intimacy), but because the place mysteriously opened
up to her the avenues of beauty and tragedy. The
Lesbian, lovely, fearless, and now dead, done to death
by the one she trusted. All this and shadowy other
things too dim to be described.

"Great Ge, how they left the place!" exclaimed
Melissa. She ran to the bed and began to toss the
pillows and beat them. "Moths, moths everywhere."

"Don't—oh, don't!" cried Chloé. "Perhaps she left
them there—just that way."

She passed her hand caressingly over the pillows,
over the embroidered covering of the bed. The bed
itself was of Greek make, shaped like a sofa—carved
on the back with a story of gods.

"May I open the chest?" whispered Chloé.

"Yes, we left almost everything."

Chloé knelt, opened it slowly, softly—an act as reverent as a libation.

"It is quite empty," she said.

"Those slaves!" exclaimed Melissa. "They'd steal the very stucco off the walls."

Chloé rose, touched the distaff, fingered the thread to the end of its length.

"Come, come," said Melissa nervously, "there are other things to see. We must get through!"

She led her into the atrium, the central room of the house, the very heart of home for Roman and for Greek. It was an inner court, roofed over save at the center, where a square opening showed the sky. Directly under this was a marble pool rightly called the impluvium, for just now the rain was pouring down into it, making all the water surface dance with leaping drops.

In one corner of this room stood the house shrine, the place of the ancient vestal hearth. Here on a large marble base stood a miniature temple, or rather temple porch, and within that a crowd of little gods, the lares and penates of the home.

Melissa and Chloé crossed over and stood reverently, the damp wind beating their garments about them.

"Is that the Lar?" whispered Chloé.

It was the central god, a curiously frivolous figure —a youth apparently dancing and prancing, holding aloft a pitcher from which he seemed to pour a libation. He was the familiar spirit of the house, its *genius,* who must be kept placated at all costs or ill luck would come. Before it even now were faded garlands and fragments of food, and on the floor, the stains of wine.

Beside the Lar stood a lesser figure, but one which outshone him like a star. It was an Apollo, slender and still, of the pre-Phidian workmanship, of marble so pure that it was almost translucent, gazing straight before him, seeing! Who shall say what he sees?

"That," whispered Melissa, "was your mother's Apollo. He really came from Eresus. One of the soldiers stole it that day. And Lævinus bought it for Chloé. She loved it and depended upon it."

But little Chloé did not hear. She had moved farther and was gazing at a portrait bust which stood on a pedestal by itself. It was the face of a young man of the Republican type; lean of cheek, austere, direct, unimaginative, yet keen. The face drew her toward it by a strange fascination.

"Who is this?" she asked.

"But that is Lævinus," said Melissa.

Chloé took a deep-drawn breath as though something were happening within her.

"Oh," she spoke to it, "I wish I had not seen you —I wish, I *wish* I had not seen you."

For now concentrated, visible, was the hate she had for Lævinus. Deep as was her reverence for her mother—even so deep went this terrible hatred for her father, until it became a horror. She stood for a moment rigid; then covered her face, cried out, sobbed, cried out again.

"Stop! Stop!" insisted Melissa, pulling her along

hastily. "Someone will hear you. They will tell Davus. Be still, can't you?"

But Chloé could not. She kept wailing and crying out while Melissa fairly bundled her back into the kitchen.

"In the name of the Twins, what's the matter?" shouted Robina. "Did Davus's boy strike her?"

"No," said Melissa. "She saw the statue of her father. He always affects her that way." Melissa thought it rather high-bred of Chloé to care so deeply.

"Well, great Jupiter, there's no use to take on like all that. Some others have had fathers bad to 'em; wailin' helps not at all."

Chloé sank down on the hearth, doubled up, sobbing.

"Well, after all, she's half starved," said Robina. She dipped a bowlful of soup from the kettle. "Here, take this. Drink it quick."

Chloé pushed it away.

"No, now you won't refuse good soup when most likely you've never had a square meal in your life. You needn't push it away; you've got to drink it!"

Robina held Chloe's shoulders firm and began to feed her with a big spoon. Chloé had to obey. The wonderful taste of the soup so surprised her that she actually caught back her sobs.

"There now, never tasted anything like that, did ye? Robina can do it. No better cook even in Rome. Now another, another."

The warmth of the soup, Robina's wholesome

roughness, were strangely quieting. Before she knew it, Chloé had drunk the bowlful and was sitting soothed and exhausted by the fire.

"Wasn't there nothin' ye liked about the house?" questioned Robina, much disappointed at the failure of her drama.

"Yes," whispered Chloé, but she could no more have told Robina about the cella-room than she could have said her prayers to her.

"What?" persisted Robina.

"There was the Apollo on the shrine," said Melissa, "the one that belonged to her mother. Oh, it is beautiful, beautiful, and it came from our dear home."

"What! That miserable little white statue that stares straight ahead, and has arms fastened to its sides?" queried Robina.

Then after a minute's thought:

"Say, ye can have that—Davus'll never know. Nobody worships there but me. I sacrifice to the Lar. He got to wailin' through the house o' nights, and he burnt my roast three days running. I had to keep him quiet."

Before Melissa could say nay, Robina had swept out of the kitchen and was back again with the precious Apollo in her hand.

"But Apollo will be angry," said the frightened Melissa. "How dare you snatch a god from the shrine?"

"I'm not snatching. He's your god, anyway. He'd

rather be with you. There's nobody to worship him there."

"But Davus, he'll surely, surely whip us."

"No, he will not. He'll not even know you were here. If he asks, I'll say I broke it when I washed the shrine. I'll wash the shrine really so he'll know it's true." Robina was beginning to believe in the breakage herself. "Davus won't dare to whip me. I'd make poor soup for a week."

As for Chloé, she was beyond believing that so divine a thing could be theirs. She reached out both hands mutely, gathered the Apollo to her bosom, and hid it in the folds of her tunic.

As they toiled up the hill toward home, she kept feeling the little hard marble figure pressed against her breast. But her inner eyes saw him continually standing before her, in the air, complete, shining, alive—as the Greeks visioned their gods.

"We'll put him in the cave part of the hut," explained Melissa, "where Davus cannot possibly find him. Maybe he will bring us some kindness out of heaven. Maybe he will see a way home."

CHAPTER 7

The Day of Saturnalia

I t was not until the Saturnalia that they saw
Robina again, or, what was more important to
Chloé, that they saw Byrsa, her daughter. Robina
came puffing up the hill (the first visit she had ever
made to them) bringing young Byrsa by the hand.

"Would you just keep her here all day?" she re-
quested. "Yes, and the night too—out of harm's way.
I'll come for her early tomorrow morning. I don't
want her down there where the shepherds are cele-
brating Saturnalia. There's no telling what might
happen. They are careering all over the place. They
have drawn down their pileus caps over their faces
so nobody can tell who's who. The wine jars are
open, and Dromo and Macar are roaring drunk already. Why, Cerberus himself couldn't keep them
out of the kitchen. They're going to elect Dromo
king for the day. Aha, he'll be a grand rex. He'll
be lord of the villa all day long."

It was plain that Robina was not so much anxious to keep Byrsa safe as to get her out of the way
so she herself would be free to take part in the fun.
Her breath was already heavy with wine, and she
was in a desperate hurry to get down the hill again.

Saturnalia was the most important holiday of the Roman year. In Rome this day the whole city would be given over to merriment and joy and wild license. Ill luck was not possible on Saturnalia. The very air was free of it. The Romans sacrificed with bare heads, being unafraid that their eyes would meet ill omens. The lordly patricians today were finding their togas too dignified for the antics of Saturnalia. They would one and all put on the short colored *synthesis* and prance about like boys; looking strangely silly and out of place. Saturn had started out a highly respectable god but like many another had fallen by the way and had become a wassailer and buffoon.

But Saturnalia was really a farm festival, first celebrated on the Latin farms, and most of all it was a festival of slaves. On this one day of the year all slaves were free. No work was required of them, even no obedience. They all donned the pileus, or liberty cap—that dream desire of every slave. For only at manumission was the pileus put on the slave; when he stood up, a free man under Roman law.

Even Davus the cruel would today lock himself in his room that he might not see their irregularities. For to punish a slave during Saturnalia was sure to bring bad luck to the punisher. These pitiful creatures on this day flung out from their cruel humiliation and had a taste of joy. Coarse and animal was that joy, for they had forgot the true kind.

At the crack of dawn Melissa and Chloé had heard the wild yells of the maskers sounding up from the valley: "Io Saturnalia, Io Saturnalia." Melissa had little use for the Roman Saturn. Of course he was a god since people worshiped him; but he was not her god, and with him she had nothing to do. Only she was grateful to him for giving her in all the year this one day of freedom.

Chloé had lain in her bed, thankful to drowse. She had no expectation save that she would all this day sit by the door of the hut, hands folded in her lap, staring into space—the dull relief from work. Then happened this marvelous thing—Robina and Byrsa appearing at this door—and Byrsa to stay. Never in all her life had she played with a girl her own age, or boy either. Melissa would not let her go to the slave quarters. They were too far away; and was not she above the slaves in rank? So Melissa pretended. So Chloé even in her few free half-hours was always alone.

But secretly she adored Byrsa. She had watched Byrsa many a day pass on the road far below and wondered if ever she might play with her. But of course Byrsa would laugh at Chloé. In the first place, Byrsa was fat, not to say lumpy. Robina's constant feeding in the kitchen had made her like a little stuffed duck. Through the dusk of her cheeks shone a deep red; her eyes were snappy and her hair frizzly. She was Carthaginian. At least Robina's ancestor had been dragged away from the smoke and ruin of Carthage, and Byrsa had the heavy Arabian features of the Phœnicians. She chattered all the time, a hoarse voice, and was always busy at something. In short, she was Chloé's ideal.

She came, carrying in one hand her own clay-jointed doll, in the other two wax tapers—*cerei,* as the customary Saturnalian gift to Melissa and Chloé.

Chloé stared at her, smiling and saying nothing, acting indeed like a child years younger than she was. Byrsa gave Melissa the tapers with the required holiday greeting, kissed her mother good-bye, walked into the hut and began to look around.

"By Pollux, it's a poor enough place," she remarked. "Mother said she knew it was; why, you sleep right against the looms on the floor. Aren't you cold o' nights? Mother said you were. And the back of the room is really a big hollow cave like a wolf would have. How dark!" She turned to Chloé. "Let's play I am the wolf of Rome and you are the twins."

"I couldn't be two," said Chloé, but at the foolish idea she laughed, a low ripple of laughter.

Melissa realized that she had never heard Chloé laugh before, not even in babyhood.

Byrsa moved about, touching everything.

"Don't touch the Apollo," called out Melissa, alarmed lest Byrsa commit that sacrilege. (What an ill-bred girl she was!)

"Saturn save us—do you call that an altar? Just two stones and a slab on top. It's not fit for a god, even that funny one you've got."

"The god makes the altar," said Melissa piously. "And Apollo regardeth the poor."

"Gods forfend, I didn't mean to call you poor."

Byrsa was quick to reply. "Mother says you are the best folk on the place. She says you ought to be the ladies in the villa."

"Why don't you two go outside?" suggested Melissa, trying not to dislike Robina's daughter. "The sun is bright."

Chloé slipped her hand into Byrsa's, and out they went. Outside was a convenient plateau, a level cliff top with a view of the world from it. To one side it sloped suddenly into a cleft. Here was Chloé's chief love—the laughing, splashing, down-plunging stream, so alive that it was not hard to know a nymph dwelt there. Byrsa only longed to get across it.

"Great Jupiter, what a forest over yonder! Let's wade through the water."

"You can in the summer," said Chloé. "But not now in the winter, when there's so much rain."

"It isn't deep; look how the rocks stick out of it."

"But there's holes," objected Chloé, "and besides, the water knocks you down."

"Oh, come along!" Byrsa had already climbed down over the stones. Now into the water.

"It's all right, 'fraid-cat." Another step! Another! Down she went to the waist in the white current. She screamed. But almost before she screamed, Chloé was in the water also. She pushed forward for a place she knew, right above Byrsa, a shallower place where she had sometimes dipped the water jar. Oh, heaven! Byrsa fell flat, head and all. Up she came spluttering and screaming. Chloé caught one wildly waving arm with both hands. She pulled, trying cautiously to step back toward shore.

"Step up here," she commanded. "Up here, I tell you." And at last Byrsa was able to lift one leg against the weight of water and to mount to the shallow ledge.

It was over in a minute. The two safe on the bank, Byrsa swearing under her breath, her garment half off and drenched.

"By Pollux, Chloé, you saved me. I'd have been dead—dead as a dog." She crouched down, trembling. "I'd have been in the dark forever and ever. Ugh, ugh!" She seemed even now in a sort of horror of darkness. But to Chloé the world was changed as if something still and smothering had suddenly moved, breathing free.

"Let's go back to Melissa. She'll dry you."

"I guess not. She'd hit me over the head. Let's go along beside the stream to the higher part." In a flash Byrsa slipped out of her dirty, soaked tunic. "There," she said, "let it dry on that rock. It felt horrid."

She began to leap like a goat over the rocks up to the forested hillside. Chloé thought she had never seen anything so beautiful. And indeed the naked brown Byrsa made a Cupid-like figure of the rounded, fat Roman sort. Into the mossy depth of the forest, in flecks of sunshine, in green shade she darted hither and yon, and Chloé followed. It was in the forest that Chloé found her treasure of the day—a dead mole.

It was a strange ecstasy, the finding of that mole—
so small with its tiny human hands, its fur, the
softest thing her fingers were ever to touch in all
her life, its little dusty snout now never more to
go delving in the earth, its mute stillness; and then
came the poignant thought that only today would it
be "playable." It was fresh. It did not smell. It was
hers! In the joy of this finding, Chloé made her first
suggestion of the day.

"Let's go down by the old olive tree and play
farm. The roots will be the walls between our farms."

They went down to an olive that was near the
hut. There each had a space between the high grey
roots which spread forth for many feet. Byrsa put
on her half-dry tunic.

"If Melissa sees me she'll hit me," she said. "Melissa hates me."

Chloé thought that so impossible as to be funny.
She laughed merrily. They gathered moss for grass,
little white stones for sheep to pasture upon it. They
built each a villa of flat stones. But the two price-
less treasures were Byrsa's doll and Chloé's mole.

"My farm is the one next door to ours," said
Byrsa. "And my doll is the grand Roman lady who
lives there. Her name is Verania."

Chloé did not know about the villa next door. She
accepted it.

"Mine is our farm," she said imitatively, "and
my mole——" She could not think of anything grand
or sweet or charming enough. "My mole is my mole,"
she finished.

Presently Melissa came, bringing the amazing loaf of bread Robina had left for Byrsa. It was a round loaf marked with radiating marks, and with it were honey and goat cheese: a feast such as Chloé had never known. Melissa brought the two tapers, struck flint and lighted them, then set them upright in two holes of the roots. They were like tiny twinkles in the December sunshine. Thus while Rome went mad with excessive romping and debauchery, while the slaves in the villa made themselves helpless with wine—two little slave girls sat beneath the tree and celebrated their Saturnalia.

CHAPTER 8

Life in the Mountain Hut

It was the last time Chloé ever saw her idolized Byrsa. About six weeks later Robina came up the hill, her hair flying loose, beating her breast, scratching her own face in an agony of grief.

"They have sold my Byrsa," she shouted. "They have sold her, sold her, sold her! Ahai! Fool that I was to keep her so fat and well. They have taken her to Neapolis, my Byrsa, to the slave market. Ahai, they will whiten her feet with chalk—they will fasten a scroll to her neck—saying, 'How well, how strong, how fine!' They will stand her upon a block. They will call aloud, 'Come buy, come buy a likely woman slave.' My Byrsa—my Byrsa!"

Melissa tried to hold her, fearing she would throw herself over the cliff. There was no comforting her; and Melissa did not try.

"Oh, if only I had not fed her so well!" the poor mother kept blaming herself. "If only I had hid her up here! If only—if only!"

Chloé came running out of the hut, her eyes wild with shock and grief.

"There now," wept Robina, "if only she'd been ugly and thin and bony like Chloé. No one'll ever sell Chloé. No one will ever buy her. But Byrsa—oh, I could kill Davus! I could kill Lævinus! 'Tis he will get the price money of my pet lamb."

"Hush! Oh, hush!" whispered Melissa. "Davus comes so quickly. He might hear."

All afternoon they held her and tried to quiet her. At nightfall they led her down to the edge of the quarters, and themselves crept back through the woods, fearful of being seen to help her.

To Chloé this was a grief unspeakable. It plunged her back into an apathy deeper than before. At night she dreamed of Byrsa, and by day, as she worked, tears for Byrsa dripped down and fell upon the wool. And all the grief harked back to Lævinus. He, the cause. He, the arch maker of evil whom she hated. She seemed to live upon this hate; or rather, she slowly died of it.

That fate like Byrsa's might befall herself did not occur to her. She took as unquestioned truth Robina's statement that she was too ugly either to be bought or sold. But Melissa feared it like an ache in her bones. Whenever she looked at Chloé, that fear struck her a blow.

So the monotonous slave life went on. The slave was *res*—not *persona*—a mere chattel. Roman slave-owners were advised to keep them at work every minute of every hour. When they were worn out, to sell them. "It is necessary," wrote Cato, "to sell old cattle, old wagons, old slaves—anything useless." Some kinder owners did not do this. But the practice was general. Melissa and Chloé received a garment each, a coarse blanket each, every *other* year. When the new was given, the old was taken away. A good pair of sandals was also bestowed every other year. Their food was meager. Davus allowed them only the fallen olives or poor ones, which had no oil. He gave them a little black bread. They also had wine. His recipe for this was memorable. It was made every year in a great vat near the vinaria:

6 gallons and 7 pints, or one amphora, of sweet wine.
2 amphoræ of sharp vinegar.
2 amphoræ of boiled must.
50 amphoræ of fresh water.
   Stir with a stick for five days, then add thirty-two gallons of *old brine*.

Such was the common recipe for slave wine. It had one advantage: it was likely to keep slaves sober forevermore. Also, as Davus said with satisfaction, "It will keep to the solstice. If any is left over it will make excellent vinegar."

As far as Chloé was concerned, it might all be made into vinegar. She could not touch it.

In such a life there was no hope; no use to save or build up. Why they lived at all is strange. They simply awoke, worked, ate, slept, and awoke again. They were indeed the machines which the Romans thought them.

Forever besetting mankind is this temptation— to make other men into machines. Always in a new form it comes to every generation, and always as disastrous to master as to slave. Slowly it is getting better, for men have grown to hate it and are battling against it. But in Roman days, after every victory, thousands of slaves were sold on the battle-field to speculators for the equivalent of eighteen cents each. They were cheap because so many died on the long march to Rome. So many committed suicide. So it was with slaves. But in the end Rome itself died because of them—rotted to the heart.

Melissa and Chloé at Caracinia Villa had a better fate than many other slaves.

Then strangely upon lives that had had no hope came a change.

Lævinus's father, old Marcus Lævinus Iberio, the grandfather of Chloé, died in Rome. Little did he suspect that his dying or the provisions of his will would affect a child far away, a child of his own blood whose existence was unknown to him. In dying he freed a number of his slaves—among them Davus. Davus, who hated the country, lost not one day in starting back to Rome. Bion, who brought the news, was vilicus in his stead.

The first that Melissa and Chloé knew of this was Bion's appearing on their cliff with Davus's guard of men.

Chloé, who was fetching water from the stream, flew in terror to her loom. Oh, if she were caught not working, what punishment would come! But Melissa rose from her loom and went out the door. She greeted Bion humbly, then she recognized him.

"Bion!" she cried. "Oh, why are you here?"

"Davus is gone," he told her. "I am vilicus now."

Melissa was speechless.

"Melissa, you have greatly changed. I did not know you."

Still Melissa could not answer. Slow tears began to steal down her face.

"Who is that working in the hut?" he asked.

"It is Chloé's child," she almost whispered. "Lævinus's child—a girl."

"Great Zeus, I did not know there was a child. Is she a slave?"

"Yes, oh, yes," broke out Melissa. "Davus has beaten her until she is like a frightened cur."

"Tell her to come out."

Melissa called at the door, and Chloé, her eyes bright with fear, came. Bion could hardly believe that this creature was connected in any way with the Lesbian Chloé he had known—this child with knotted hanging locks, pallid cheeks, expressionless face.

He did not speak for a moment. Then, as if embarrassed, he said:

"Cannot she sit in the sun for a while? It is so warm and fresh. She—I don't like her paleness."

"She can do what you command," said Melissa, her voice trembling with unbelief.

Chloé did the best thing in the world. She lifted her big eyes and met Bion's.

"You speak Greek," she murmured. "You speak our own Island Greek. You are a Lesbian." The sound of the beloved tongue made her forget all else.

"No, I am a Bœotian," he answered, "but it is the same thing. Bœotians and Lesbians are one blood."

Thus it was in the underworld of slavery, that kin met kin, in far-off stranger-lands.

After he was gone Melissa, half crying, half laughing with joy, tried to explain to the confused Chloé.

"He is Bion the Bœotian. . . . Yes, he is a slave. It was he that Lævinus long ago used to put in charge of the farm whenever he went away. Bion remembers the days of our honor. He knew your mother as *matrona*. Davus sent him away before you were born. . . . Yes, of course he speaks our Æolic— all Bœotians do. Oh, my darling, my darling—he is Greek and has the human heart of a Greek. He will be kind to us. Davus is gone. Don't you understand? —Davus is gone for good."

But Chloé did not understand. Cruelty had always been in her life, and she could not imagine life without it. Now as the days went on she did not have to work all the hours of daylight. But the cessation from work meant only a hopeless sitting in front of the hut. There was nothing that she wanted to do. The very let-up of active tragedy seemed to deprive life of its only force. Despair in the old is a grievous thing, but not so bad as despair in the young. The young have no weapons, no remembrances of evils overcome, nor of evils endured. They have no muscle-hardness from old battles. They see only what is present, and they believe it to be forever. And *they are very sure*. Besides, joy and up-springing are the right of youth, and without it youth falls to the ground.

Melissa was frightened. She went to the forest and

gathered boughs of bay, Apollo's daphne tree. With
these she wove an arch over their small marble Apollo.
At every meal Melissa put some fragment on the
altar—no matter how hungry they were. She poured
out a little wine before him.

"O Apollon," she prayed, "my gift is not great. It
is not the right gift. But accept thou our gift. Save
Chloé. Save Chloé."

Chloé stood with her at the altar, but she did not
pray. As for Apollo, he stood gazing dreamily into
the darkness of the hut, so silent, so undisturbed.

But Apollo answered the prayer. So Melissa believed. Was it not the seventh of the month, Apollo's
especial day when it happened—the marvelous thing?
Was not Apollo from eld the tender guardian of
flocks?

Melissa had gone down to the villa for more wool.
Chloé would not go. She was too tired, and besides,
the quarters only made her remember Byrsa again.
Melissa was returning along the path which led to
the pastures, when she met Myntas, the great six-
and-a-half-foot Gaul, carrying a goat.

"What of the goat?" Melissa asked in the slave-
jargon Latin she had learned.

Myntas clicked his tongue regretfully.

"She fell and broke her leg, and the kid, too, will
die. No other goat will nourish it. I am taking the
goat to the kitchen door to kill her."

And just then—Apollo of flocks being present—
Bion came by in the path.

Melissa threw herself at his feet with all the aban-
don that Lesbians knew.

"Oh, Bion, give me the goat. I will tend it and
cure it. Chloé's child is dying—no less. With milk
perhaps she will live. She refuses the slave food. Oh,
Bion, give me the goat."

Bion did not hesitate. He gave her the goat at
once. He even slipped a coin into Myntas's hand to
appease him for loss of the meat, and bade him
carry the goat up the hill.

"Take the kid, too," he commanded. "I wouldn't
be surprised if Melissa should save them both."

So they came toiling up the path. Chloé, sitting
by the hut, saw their two heads appear above the
cliff, Myntas carrying the goat, Melissa the kid.
Chloé rose, slightly interested.

"Go quick, child," commanded Melissa, "get me a
smooth strong stick; see now, larger and stronger
than the poor broken leg. And a thick piece of yarn
to bind it on. Aye, and a jar of fresh water to wash
the leg."

Chloe went out obediently. When she returned,
there was the goat lying in the corner of the hut, the
kid beside her. The splint was too short. Melissa
went out to find another.

"If she tries to get up, catch her by the horns
and cry out for me," she commanded.

But the goat did not try to rise. She lay there in
animal patience under suffering and satisfied to have
her kid with her.

Chloé crouched by her. Once she put out her

hand and touched the hairy flank. But the goat raised her head with eyes rolling alarmedly.

"Oh, I won't touch you again," Chloé explained, frightened. "Please lie still." She spoke to it as to an equal.

Melissa returned. She washed the wounded leg; she bound it straight between two flattish sticks.

"What shall we call her?" she questioned the silent Chloé. Chloé thought intently.

"Let's call her Sappho, after the dearest one in our Isle." She pronounced the word "Psappha" as all Lesbians did.

Melissa thought it strangely disrespectful to call a goat after the famed lyrist. But it did not occur to Chloé that a goat was not as respectable as a poetess.

"And the baby we will call Cleis," she added, "because she was Psappha's daughter. But how will Psappha crop the grass when she cannot walk?"

"You will go up to the high meadow and gather grass for her. I will have to get withes and make you a basket. But tomorrow you will just carry the grass in your arms."

"Let me help make the basket, too," pleaded Chloé.

"Two cannot work upon a basket," answered Melissa.

They went to sleep in the hut—goats and women together. In the night Melissa heard a strange step.

"Chloé—where are you going?"

"Psappha might be hungry," came Chloé's shivery voice. "It is quite light with the moon. I could go up to the meadow now."

"Lie down again, child. Psappha will do quite well until day," commanded Melissa.

But at the first peep of the sun, Chloé was clambering up to a level meadow above the hut. She pulled and pulled the grass, wet up to her elbows with dew. She came back with a great arm full. As soon as Psappha had eaten, she was off again. She made the trip again and again—she who had been too weak to go down to the villa.

In the afternoon, when Melissa had fetched the withes from a farm hedge, Chloé sat by her with hands so instinctively outstretched to the work that Melissa gave it to her and showed her the basket-weaving. To her surprise, after several attempts, Chloé did the work firm and true.

"Psappha makes so much to do," she said contentedly.

Next morning Chloé, sleeping on the floor by her loom, was awakened by a warm sweet breath in her face, and opened her eyes to see the kid leaning over her with wondering curiosity. Now among all young animals under heaven the kid is the most appealing. A lamb is almost its equal; but a lamb lacks a certain alertness and illusive meaning. Violets at dawn, crocuses out of the snow—all things flower-like and lovely—these are its ilk. Besides, a kid is a joke. To see one is to laugh aloud with sudden pleasure. And so Chloé laughed. She seized the little thing and drew it to her. The rising sun lay in level gold on the hut floor. She sprang up with the kid in her arms and ran out of doors with it. It escaped from her, she caught it again, raining kisses on its head. Again it wiggled free. This was the first of the romps of Chloé and Cleis, in which Cleis soon knew the game quite as well as Chloé herself.

Before long Psappha could walk enough to crop the grass near the house. Then Melissa milked her and gave Chloé her first cupful.

"But it belongs to Cleis!" Chloé objected.

"The god of flocks always provides enough for beasts and men," said Melissa.

And then, to cap all joys, Psappha and Cleis must be led up to the high pasture and Chloé must do the leading; every morning, in sunshine or rain, climbing up over the rocks and moss and gnarled roots, with the animals following for love of her. Every evening Chloé made the ascent again, calling and hunting for them—always a little anxious lest they had wandered. Yet always finding them at last.

CHAPTER 9

Riches

It is strange how people will try to mend their lives when the garment is torn to shreds. It is strange, too, how life's garment, unlike human weaving, grows whole with the mending. It is as if some invisible kindness out of the air had set to work with you— here a little and there a little. So it was when Melissa brought the goats into the hut.

These happenings were very slight—which meant so much to the two slaves.

One day Chloé returned from her high pasture with some red berries, asking if they were good to eat.

"Indeed no!" answered Melissa. "But they will dye anything a beautiful crimson. They will dye crimson, but also blue according as you use them."

So Chloé made a basket of sweet grass with a startling crimson border, baskets with patterns of red and natural yellow—of blue and buff. Her patterns were Greek and had the instinctive Greek beauty. Bion saw the baskets and said Chloé might make them for market. Thus changing from her eternal work at the loom.

Another day Chloé, sitting in the sunshine, was weaving a basket of osiers which looked like a little dome.

"Oh, it is shaped like a hive," cried Melissa. "Let us make it into a hive. Perhaps Apollo will send us bees."

So they made a hive, covering the basket with wet clay—which they baked in the sun, leaving a tiny door for those wise small tribes to enter. And surely Apollo knew of their so doing, for only a few weeks later Chloé, returning from the pasture, heard a strange booming noise, and there a low branch of a beech tree was well-nigh breaking with the weight of a great brown ball of bees. They seemed no longer individuals but a solid mass of life. Chloé broke the branch. It did not disturb them. They seemed possessed with some strange, absorbing project of their own. She carried them, branch and all, carefully to the hut.

"Oh, Melissa," she called, "they have come! Apollo has sent them."

She began with her bare hands to take off handfuls of them and put them into the hive.

"Have a care!" cried Melissa. "They will sting you horribly."

But they stung her not at all—crawling contentedly over her arms to the elbows or buzzing forth from the hive again.

"Wait, wait," said Melissa. She covered her head and peeped fearfully at them. "We must see if you have their king.* For if they have him they are perfectly happy—but if not they will wander off and die. For they love him devotedly."

"Oh, see, here is one bee quite different from the others—so large and with such stubby wings!" said Chloé, tenderly holding the creature in her palm.

"It is the king—yes—the king. Put him in quickly. Now all will follow him into the hive."

And so it was. Soon the hive was humming like a busy city. It had been set on a flat rock by the stream and under the olive. For bees love pure water and the olive is their favorite tree.

"And you know," chattered Melissa happily, "that if our hive were cluttered with old wax, they would clean it all out; for they are neater than we are. You would find the refuse tomorrow morning all thrown away out the door. I am glad that the bed of thyme grows below the cliff, for that they love. But they can find what flowers they wish, though they be miles away; and they know the way home. Ah, even now they are building their cells of wax. You know it was they who made the first temple of Apollo at Delphi—a tiny temple all of golden wax. How pretty it must have been, shining in the sun! And it was they who put honey on Pindar's lips and gave him the divine gift of song. Honey and song are one. And you know when the Pleiades rise we have the right to take their honey; and again when they set. We must watch the stars."

* Note. I have taken the lore about the bees from Virgil. He is not quoted because he was not yet born. The ancients thought the queen bee was a king.—C.D.S.

So Melissa chattered on, mixing legend and truth. But no legend can be so wonderful as the truth about the bees.

One afternoon Robina came up to see if it were true concerning the goats. Robina was older and soberer than she had been. She was always hoping that some news might come of her lost Byrsa—always knowing that such a chance was like finding a small jewel in a wheat field. She had a son, Geta, who was much comfort to her.

"He's the finest shepherd of the lot," she bragged of him. "He can build the best sheepfolds. Bion says if he sold every man on the farm he wouldn't sell him. Oh, I hope it's true."

She was charmed with Psappha. "And to think she had a broken leg and came so near making soup in my pot! Why, she's the strongest-looking goat I've seen, and the white kid is growing nicely. Soon two goats. It's hardly believable. Oh, suppose"—Robina was a person of unquenchable hope—"suppose Psappha has twins next spring and the kid has her first. You'd have five goats—by Pollux, you would be rich!"

"We are rich now," spoke Melissa. She took Robina down to the stream, where in the coolness stood two earthen bowls of milk.

"See, I can offer hospitality," she added, dipping a cupful for Robina. "And you must taste our cheese and our honey."

Chloé left her weaving to sit by Robina and listen to the news. Robina lifted both hands at sight of her.

"Why, what's struck the child?" she cried. "She's grown tall. She's a woman grown. Not very fat—but, gods, she begins to look decent. That milk must have magic in it."

"Psappha is all magic," laughed Chloé.

But Robina was quite horrified at their keeping the goats in the hut.

"Of course everybody does it," she said elegantly. "But me—I don't like it at all, they smell so. Perhaps I've got used to the kitchen, where Lævinus never liked them about." She began looking around for something.

"As I'm alive there's a good cave in the cliff not a stone's throw from your house," she said. "You must put them in there."

"Oh, but we are afraid," objected Chloé. "Suppose a wolf should get them—suppose they should wander away. Besides, I love them near."

"Geta will come up and fix you," went on Robina. "He'll build a stone wall across the cave mouth, and a wicket gate that no wolf can get by. Then you'll have a sheepfold."

And, sure enough, next day came Geta bearing a large two-handled jar, a gift from Robina.

"Mother said both your milk bowls were broken," he explained. "And one of them surely leaks. This will hold the milk."

He was a thickset youth with muscles in his arms like ropes. He had Byrsa's same frizzy hair and was dressed in a single abbreviated tunic of sheepskin, wool-out. It hung on one shoulder and left his chest bare, a chest as hairy as the goats he tended. Straightway he fell to work, lifting great stones and building them in front of the cave so cleverly that there was not a crevice between them. He planted gateposts and wove a strong gate of boughs with willow hinges.

"There," he said proudly. "That'll keep your five goats safe when you have 'em."

He made a broom of twigs. "And you, Chloé, must sweep out the hut so it won't be so much like a stable."

But Melissa had already seized the broom and was sweeping everywhere.

"We were so miserable we had gotten to be like animals," she muttered. "You are a good man, Geta."

Next day, to their surprise, he came again and without a word began to set two posts in front of the hut, buttressing them with stones. Over the posts he built a light roof of woven twigs, very close and smooth. Toward evening the porch was done.

"It will almost turn rain," he said proudly. "But if it doesn't, daub it with clay." Then he brought Chloé's loom out to the porch.

"See how fine you can weave out here in the sunshine," he remarked. "When it's too windy for the threads, you and Melissa can carry it in. But out of doors is best. Me—I couldn't live in that dark hut."

Chloé's face blushed with pleasure.

"And now," he added, "I've done a lot o' work for you, and you are to give me a kiss."

He drew her to him and gave her cheek a sounding smack.

But Chloé liked this part of his day's work—not at all!

CHAPTER 10

The Forest

We folk of the modern day can, with a touch of the finger, flash a whole city into light; we can plunge through clouds faster than any bird; we can soar above the very atmosphere of earth.

But we have lost the sweet informing companionship of animals which was the daily life of men of old. Animals as pets are not the same. They are not these ancient vital companions. These ancient animals were in equal partnership with men, gave as much as they took—gave sometimes more. They carried men on their journeys, they gave them food, they clothed them. Life could not go on without them; and with them, life was sweet, warm, responsive. No one who has not seen animals leading their individual lives in pasture, field, or byre can possibly guess how rich in happenings, friendships, humorous schemes and contrivings their lives are.

Chloé and Melissa had still those long dull hours of work, ever throwing the pitiless shuttle through the warp. But often as they sat at the looms in front of the hut, Cleis would be leaping and goat-dancing on the grass, quite as if she meant to amuse. Psappha would be calling to be milked; the bees would rush by in arrowlike flight. Once they threatened to swarm—came pouring and booming out of the hive; and Chloé and Melissa had to beat with sticks, shout, clap their hands to arrest them. And later they had to find the rival "king" and make a new hive for "him" and "his" revolutionary followers. The bees made busy hours for humans as well as for themselves. Evening after evening in the spring Chloé would sit watching the great expanse of eastern sky for the first glimpse of those diamond twinklers, the Pleiades, so she might open the hive.

"Do you suppose the Pleiades know about the honey?" she wondered. "Or do they just rise and not care?"

"Many stars are gods," said Melissa wisely, "and see what they will."

Yes, life was busy and companioned, with these new friends so close to earth, and the far ones in the heavens.

But the happiest thing of all for Chloé was a new-found freedom in the forest. It happened as if by accident one spring day when the snows of winter had ceased. Chloé these days did her weaving much more swiftly. The cruelty of Davus, which had tangled her threads with evil, was all smoothed away by Bion's kindness. Chloé now wove deftly, large smooth fabrics for togas, for couch coverings. She even embroidered the last with colored thread. She often finished what Bion required in three quarters of a day. Then she was free to go.

On this spring afternoon she suddenly wished to

cross the stream. The forest on the far side had always seemed more beautiful than the one near by, with nobler trees and deeper moss. And this afternoon the forget-me-nots at the stream's edge were a new profusion, the anemones and violets glimpsed beyond were like a call. She stepped into the stream, but the rushing current, augmented by the rains, drove her back. She climbed the hill to where the stream was narrower and full of rocks. But here the rocks were all overwhelmed, the water leaping white into the air.

Suddenly she caught sight of a pliant grapevine hanging from a beech. She grasped it in her hands. Did she dare? If she failed to leap the chasm, the stream was wild enough to drown her.

She knelt by the stream, touched the hurrying water with her hands, and made invocation to the nymph of that fountain. Then she felt safe. She caught the vine again, ran back as far as she could, ran forward—made the leap!

She landed in a heap on the other side, on stones which did not fail to bruise her, stones so steep and slippery with slimy moss that it was only by clinging to some bare roots that she kept from sliding back into the depth.

But she thought of none of these things. She was free in a new place. She had discovered a new country. She went forward, marveling. The trees stood in great silence, and all the air was shot through with emerald light. There were spruces and firs, with, here and there, large-girthed oaks which pushed these lesser ones back and made a space for themselves to grow. They seemed to know that Zeus was their father.

A forest in vale or flat country hems men in, encloses them, both mind and body, in a thickset circle. But a mountain forest—a forest on a slope—is different. Always it gives glimpses of far valleys, terrorizing edges of cliff with only the sky to meet it, and the profound below. Light suddenly floods the forest, and the spirit of all space is there. A level forest is the abode of lesser spirits, but a mountain slope lets in the great ones—Hermes, Apollo—Zeus himself.

She spent an hour exploring beauties—glades unexpected, with wet flowers in their depths, lengths of limestone cliff, forest-enclosed, and showing here and there a cave where water trickled. She was a little afraid of the caves, for nymphs might dwell there, and "nymphs are dangerous." At the mouth of one was a little broken shrine, so she was certified of that one. She wished she could read the inscription and fingered the letters timidly before she hurried away. The forest was all clamber up and down, until she was tired out. She came to an opening. The forest was suddenly halted by sheer space—space of air, space of sky, space of a far-stretched valley—where things grew tiny like toys. The cliff edge stood sharp, absolute.

"I am glad Cleis is not here," Chloé thought. "She might tumble over the edge." She was quite unafraid for herself. She lay down on the ground with a sigh, very tired. She did not know what made her so light of heart in this place. She did not know (for we seldom recognize such mental backgrounds) that in the hut, at her weaving, she was constantly nursing her hatred for Lævinus. It was there like a shadow over all her thinking. Her mother's grave within sight, her forced labor with no reward— "Lævinus, the cause! Lævinus, the cause!" Here, strangely, that shadow lifted. Of its own accord it lifted and left her free, so youth came to her.

She looked out over the valley. An eagle was floating wing-still across the space. How lovely to be so high, so sure to reach the goal. The eagle was making for a great jutting cliff. There was its nest. Now, since the sun happened to be just right, Chloé could see it alight, accurate and sure, with wings stretched high above its back, and talons thrust down to grasp the rocks. There, the thing was done!

Chloé lay drowsing "softly at the gate of dreams." Now far to the right where the ground was steep with piled-up talus, she saw someone approaching. She sat up to see better. Yes, someone coming up toward her, a small far-off figure finding pathway among the low juniper bushes. An excitement came over Chloé, that she should meet a stranger. She had met so few—indeed none—in her life. And something told her that this one was no slave. She climbed so lightly among the stones—a young girl her own age. Now she was quite near. What a face! Such dreamy thoughtfulness and a little anxiety, too—as though making an effort to be mortally visible. But Chloé could see her. Her form, faintly rosy, shone through her long garment, which was transparent, iridescent and delicately stiff like a May fly's wing. Chloé's excitement gave place to a serene peace like space itself—a surety of presence and protection. She knew it was a nymph, the nymph of that cave whom she had been afraid of. The nymph had been away. She was coming back to her home.

Now on the very cliff she paused; she bent down as a bough bends in the wind. No—not to touch Chloé herself, but to touch and caress a mother rabbit that had hopped out of its covert softly to her very feet. The rabbit had three little ones. The nymph touched each one on the head. Then she looked at Chloé. How that smile went through to Chloé's inmost mind!

Then she rose erect and walked onward, so near that the May-fly garment swept the grass at Chloé's side, but made no sound.

She was gone! Chloé felt sorry for the rabbit. It looked so disappointed. Nymphs were the special protectors of woodland creatures and their young. The rabbit began to hop forlornly toward Chloé as if for comfort. Its cold, twitchy nose touched Chloé's hand.

With a start Chloé awoke. But no, she had not been asleep. There was the rabbit and its three little ones. It had indeed touched her hand. At Chloé's start it hopped two hops away. Not far. It was not afraid. Who could be afraid after the presence of a goddess? The rabbit was not more real than the nymph—no, not more real. Had not the nymph touched its head just now? Had she not touched

Chloé, too, with that more intimate touch of love?

Chloé scrambled to her feet, found her way back through the wood with strange, unweighted step, as if floating upon the power of her inner delight and dream. She swung across the brook, ran down the other side, and came bursting into the hut.

"Melissa, Melissa!" she called. "I have seen a nymph. I have seen a nymph of the wood. She lives in a cave and was on her way home."

CHAPTER 11

Songs That Move the Heart of Shaken Heaven

Songs that move the heart of shaken heaven,
Songs that break the heart of earth with pity,
Sappho—thy singing.
A paraphrase from Swinburne's Sapphics

After this Chloé went into the wood every day. If she had a spare hour she went, for a half-hour, a few moments. She went in shine or rain, in the dense fog of the mountains. Once a cloud so enveloped her that she could not find her way home and had to stay the night through. Melissa was frightened. But Chloé was frightened not at all. Who could be afraid when the kind nymph was there? Chloé crept into a hollow oak and slept as rabbits and chipmunks sleep. She had another name for the forest. She called it φυγή (escape). Here she escaped from slave bondage, from work and the thought of work. Here she was free. Melissa was at first worried over this unnatural solitude for her darling. She feared some strange possession by the nymph, some snatching away into invisibility, or god-madness of the mind. But when she saw how tall and rosy Chloé was growing, she could not fear for her. She could only brave the loneliness which Chloé's absence left to her in the hut.

Chloé never entered her forest by wading the brook. Even when the droughts of summer made it perfectly easy to cross right at hut-side. She always climbed up to the same place and swung across by her grapevine. And so it came to pass that what had at first been a dangerous venture became an easeful flight. She took her start from farther back, swung into the air in a great arc, and landed, not bruised or falling, but tiptoe, and perfectly sure—as an alighting swallow. Sometimes she sang as she made the leap, as certain few songbirds do—singing in flight.

It was this leap rather than the forest ramble which made Chloé grow tall—tall and very slender. But her hands had a grasp of iron, and her arms, now delicately rounded, had hidden in them the muscles of a strong boy. The leap was hot work—for she would leap back and forth until she was tired and breathless. Then she would strip off her brown slave tunic, dip herself in the waterfall. Chloé was Roman in her love of water—for no race in the world's history has loved water and mere bathing as they. Besides, a waterfall appeals perhaps as nothing else in nature—so white, so strangely fragrant, so bountifully flowing from an eternal source which we somehow feel is our Source too.

Self-respect was not easy to acquire for one who had to work so many hours without reward, and who yet remembered whippings in her dreams. But self-

respect began to show in Chloé, in the way she
held her head and her whole body erect. She brushed
and cared for her hair, tried to make it lie straight.
It rippled back from her temples in the way so common among the Greeks and which the sculptors gave
to the Lady Hera.

"Does it look like Byrsa's?" she asked Melissa
longingly.

"No, child," answered Melissa, "but it will do
very well."

Day by day Chloé wove at the loom more skillfully, beginning to care for the work now that she
did it so well. She and Melissa were the best weavers
on the farm. All the finest wool was given to their
care. The garments from their looms were not sold
in the market but reserved for Lævinus's own household, so that Chloé's half-brother in Rome, her little
sister, and Lævinus himself, though they knew it not,
wore clothes that were the creation of Chloé's swift
fingers.

Of course none of this happy development would
have been possible but for the over-arching kindness
of Bion. He was a thorough farmer, easy-going, yet
producing results through knowledge gained by generations on the soil. Bion felt deeply his Æolic kin-
ship to Melissa and Chloé. In the heavy winter
which this year visited the mountains, he would often
come up the hill with his men to "dig them out"
of the hut. The snow drifting down from the slopes
above was four or five feet deep. He would shovel

out a great circle in front of the hut to set them wholly free. Often he would find a narrow canyon already dug by Chloé and Melissa—to their precious cave of goats. Not only must these dear friends be fed and cared for, but there in the cave Melissa kept their store of fagots and wood. Bion would have none of this wood. "Woman's gathering," he called it. He and his men would fell sizable trees, would pile up great logs in the cleared space outside the hut and set them afire to burn for days. The morrow of a heavy snow like this was sure to be bitter. Then Chloé would light an additional fire far back in the rock part of the hut. It filled the room with blinding smoke, in which they sat weeping. There was little weaving to be done on such a day. Chloé, running out to get her breath or to milk the goats, would see below that far, serene vale of whiteness, with blue shadows of peak or forest lying across it. How still it slept, withdrawn and pure! In after years, in the closeness and heat of Rome, Chloé was to remember this and refresh her inner mind. But now she thought not of it, being intent upon the goats. Robina's prophecy had been fulfilled. There were indeed five goats now, and a sheep which Melissa had received in exchange for a kid. Melissa sheared the sheep and wove the wool into a cloak for herself and a white tunic for Chloé. But she never let the slaves know this—not even Robina—for fear of jealousy. Ah, they were rich indeed.

As the spring of this year advanced, Bion did not

forget them. He would come up in the evening after his work was done and sit with Melissa to talk about his home in Bœotia. He told how each little field was planted and what it was good for, quoting often the wisdom of Hesiod. Chloé would sit near, waiting for him to come to better things. For Bion was sure to come at last to his beloved Bœotian Pindar. It was strange about Pindar; even when Chloé cared little about the subject, the peculiar strength of Pindar's vision would sweep her like a "gale of song."

Then Melissa would sing, perhaps a shepherd song of Lesbos, perhaps a song of Sappho herself. Chloé would hum with her, for she knew by heart all that Melissa knew. And gradually, as she grew more courageous and self-forgetting, Chloé would sing aloud quite as Melissa sang.

They chose the moon's nights for their singing. Once as they sang that old Sappho Song,

"The moon rose full, and women stood as though about an altar,"

the actual moon floated softly as a blown bubble up over a mountain edge and flooded the whole valley with silver. Chloé began to sing so sweetly that Melissa stopped and let her sing on alone as the moon moved alone in the sky. Her voice was high and flute-like as a boy's, unshaken by emotion, piercing beyond emotion in pure flight.

Next day, when Chloé was not near, Bion said:

"She will be a beautiful singer, Melissa. Will that be well for her or ill?"

"Bion, I do not know," Melissa answered anxiously. "It seems whatever she is now, or does, is only danger. Oh, if she should be sold as a slave singer in Rome I would rather she would die."

"Perhaps Geta will marry her," suggested Bion.

"Oh, no, no. Geta is so rough. I do not think she could endure Geta." Then, after a pause: "Bion, I have sometimes thought *you* might accept Chloé. Would you?"

Bion stirred uneasily.

"No, I have another plan." (Melissa wondered whether he had a wife in Rome.)

"But I have a brother in Rome," said Bion. "He has lost his wife. I think he would marry Chloé."

"But that would take Chloé away to Rome."

"No, I would try to get Lævinus to send him to the farm."

"Is your brother younger than you?"

"No, he is older, quite settled. It would be a fine match."

Neither Melissa nor Bion thought that Chloé might object to marrying a man more than twice her age. Such slave marriages were not considered legal by the Romans, but the slaves so regarded them. And many such marriages lasted faithfully through a lifetime and were tenderly recorded on slave tombstones.

CHAPTER 12

The Wild Rider

The fields stood ripe to the harvest, and upon them was the mood of waiting to give and to be given. The day of the ancient Italian festival, the most ancient of all, had arrived—the festival of Ceres, or Keri, as the country people called her. The Romans said that Ceres was the same as Demeter. This was not true. Ceres was only a dim sense of growth from the soil and man's response to that mystery with thankfulness and awe.

But long ago the worship of Ceres had been overlaid by the worship of Demeter, that vivid goddess brought over to Italy by the Greeks of Magna Græca. Now the two goddesses were indissolubly one. The country people of the Villa Caracinia might worship Keri in the Latin fashion, but Bion, Melissa, and Chloé worshiped their own Demeter.

As they came down the hill path to the fields their minds were filled with the beautiful old stories of the Corn Mother, that very dearness-of-motherhood, embodied in the generous, wide-breasted form of Demeter. Had not the goddess all winter been grieving for her lost daughter, Persephone? Could they not feel her grief in the bitterness of the air, the hardness of earth, and the disappearance of all flowering things? And now only look—the flowers stood by every path where no human hand had tended them. Demeter's hand had been there—hers only. Chloé this morning was picturing intensely the lone mother, Demeter, where she sat in the small open temple at Eleusis. Chloé could imagine the goddess lifting her face of sorrow. There through the bare fields was coming a tender maiden—Persephone— alive again, given back by Hades himself. It could be none other, for see how the path she treads through the dry meadow is made a path of bloom. Then the arms of Demeter spread wide for her child. Persephone runs into that sweet enfolding. And as the two goddesses weep together for joy the fields grow green. Flowers, flowers are everywhere, even as they are now in the Samnian hills. Demeter-Chloé is the name of Demeter now. Chloé, the tender first green of leaves in spring, for which Chloé herself was named. Chloé wondered wistfully if her own dear Chloé-mother would wait for her in the mysterious Unseen, wait as Demeter waited and so enfold her.

At the foot of the hill Robina, Geta, all the people of the Villa formed a procession and so moved onward to the fields. Processions are natural in Italy.

"So long as the cloud shadows move in slow, lustral procession over the hollow of the hills."

Thus Virgil in these same Apennines was to write as he thought of the religious processions of his people. And today in Italy the same cloud shadows of human life move toward the churches in country and in town.

They reached the fields—the still, outspread gold of wheat breathing a fragrance more delicate than any garden's. Who would dare to put in the first sickle, to disturb this perfect gift of Mystery? Surely not anyone in that ancient procession, until first the goddess had been propitiated. They therefore marched about the field purifying it in silence—lustration, as they called it. They came to an altar at the field's edge. Then happened what was so common in ancient worship that everybody took it for granted—that is, everybody but Chloé.

She had witnessed so few festivals—none in her early childhood. The whole thing was as strange to her as it was not to Melissa or to anyone else in the company.

They made a blood sacrifice. A large sow was brought protesting to the altar. Of course she did not want to die, that sow—she wanted to live and feed her little ones. Chloé knew that, but nobody else seemed to know or care. They pierced the sow to the heart, and with a great scream she died. The necessary blood spilled and spurted on the altar—soiled already with many a former sacrifice. We who have had clean altars for almost two thousand years can in no wise enter into the feelings of these worshipers. To some it was the earnest of an answer from the god, who must give gift for gift; to others it was the satisfaction of witnessing cruelty, to others the surety of a meal of fresh meat, to yet others the deep, strange symbolism of death.

To Chloé it was none of these things. She screamed aloud when the animal screamed. She hid her face from the agony of the pig, who, with the goats at home, the rabbit in the forest, the bird upon the bough, was her friend. Geta, who had managed to be next her, was vastly amused. He seized her hands and pulled them down. But she tore them away from him. She did not speak, nor did Geta; for silence must be kept at sacrifice. Fortunately no one had noted Chloé's scream (at least no one but Geta), else all the sacrifice would have to be done over again.

Now Bion entered the field—cut the first sacred sickleful and laid it on the altar as an offering to the Corn Mother. Then the reapers followed, and swung their glistening sickles into the gold. They bent downward, rising with a half-turn as they laid the cut grain on the ground. The sickles cut with a long, strange whisper of sound. But soon you could not hear the whisper for the rhythmic chanting of the reapers.

At noon the happy procession marched back again to slave quarters for the sacrificial feast. Melissa, Chloé, Bion, and others had the privilege of the kitchen. Here Geta made merry over Chloé's social mistake.

"Ahai! Can ye believe it? She screamed just exactly in tune with the pig. Did you ever hear of such a country jake? You'd think she never had been at a festival before. Never mind, Chloé, come and live at quarters with me and I'll teach ye better manners." All this with nudges and pokes at Chloé.

"Keep still, will ye?" admonished Robina. One could see she was not well pleased with Geta's form of courting. To hold Chloé up to ridicule was his way of making love.

"Well," said Robina informatively, "the people next door at the Villa Cornelia have come down for the harvest festival. Not the old Master—he never comes. But the young master, Aulus Cornelius, and the mistress, Verania, his mother. And two dear little girls. They're glad as goats to be in the country. Me —I don't see how anybody stands Rome when the heat comes on."

Robina was sweating profusely as she basted the pork. A slave turned the spit. The smell of the meat filled the air and made everybody hungry. But hungry or not, they would have to wait an hour for the meat to be done.

"Geta," commanded Robina, "stop your nonsense, pulling Chloé about like that. Go out now and get me some more sage and rosemary from my vegetable patch down the hill. You know the bed."

Geta, with a final poke at Chloé, dashed off. Instantly Chloé hid behind a group of slaves who were baking the loaves. No one noticed her. They were too fascinated with the cooking. She could not bear Geta today. She hated him. He had touched her, and touched her again. She could feel yet the places of his touch. He might even kiss her before the day was done. No, no—he should not do that! She escaped into the deserted house, into the atrium. Then out into the sunny tangled garden beyond. Here she could bury herself in a yew hedge and no one would find her. How quiet the garden was, and most of all how quiet the Athena who stood guardian of the place, not goddess of Wisdom but goddess of Spinning. Lævinus had set her there to symbolize the spinning industry of the farm. Chloé came close to the statue, a lovely Greek creation, not new but centuries old. Clad as Athena was always in the long chiton with straight stiff folds to her feet, she held the distaff, and her outstretched hand deftly twisting the invisible thread might have been Chloé's own. Happy goddess! Pure, virginal. No one ever kissed her against her will, or touched her when she wished not to be touched. Chloé crouched close to Athena's feet.

"Guard me and help me, Athena Spinner," she whispered. "See how I weave every day—hours upon hours for thee. And it was thou who brought weaving to the earth."

She began to pull away the weeds from the statue base, the vines that had twined about the very form of the goddess.

"Guard me," she kept whispering. "I will bring thee an olive branch. I will give thee my spindle if only Bion will let me have another."

The pulling of the vines, the quiet face of Athena calmed Chloé. When she had quite freed the statue of such growth, she walked onward to the end of the garden toward a break in the wall.

"If I go beyond the wall, Geta can never find me," she thought. She looked through the gap.

Far below was a glimpse of the Villa Cornelia hidden in trees; but nearer, quite at the base of Chloé's hill where she stood, was the Cornelian horse pasture. And there—there were people! The grooms bringing out the horses—the lovely Lady Verania herself clothed in white, and two little girls younger than Chloé—clothed in white also. Surely they were not to ride the horses. No, for now out from the villa porch ran a youth older than Chloé—perhaps seventeen years old. He lifted his right hand to his mother —the Roman greeting. Then the groom had scarce brought the horse into place when he leaped—one beautiful clear vault from the ground—upon the horse's back. The horse sprang away as if the touch of the young man had frightened him into life, away, away—in a great circle about the field—the boy's body answering to the gallop in lovely, wild rhythm, his tunic fluttering from his shoulders. Every time he passed the Lady Verania and the little girls he gave a delighted shout, and they held out their arms to him, as if frightened that he should go so fast—yet happy, too.

Chloé was not frightened. She knew he could never fall. The horse loved him too well. Any horse would love such a rider. Now the groom came running out with another horse. The young man's horse slowed to meet the second one. Then as the two horses gal-

loped side by side, the young man got to his feet on
his horse's back, then lightly leaped over upon the
second horse. Chloé shouted aloud. No one could hear
her so far away. But she could hear faintly the shouts
of the little girls and the groom. Surely no one in
the whole world could ride like this. It was he alone,
Aulus Cornelius, who could ride so.

Chloé did not know that this was the new popular
sport in Rome. At first it was practised only by pro-
fessionals in the arena. They were called *desultors*
and often rode four horses abreast. Aulus was satisfied with two horses, and his audience—the known
one in the pasture, and the unknown on the hilltop—
were satisfied beyond measure with his riding. He
dashed about the pasture for perhaps fifteen minutes,
springing from one horse to the other. Then, waving
his mother farewell, the young Cornelius galloped
off, out the pasture gate and down the road to ride
alone. The Lady Verania watched him until he dis-
appeared. Then she made a curious little beckoning
motion in the air with her right hand. This was calling down blessings from the hidden divine ones upon
her son. Instinctively Chloé reached up her right
hand and beckoned a blessing too. She was so full
of happiness, so filled, body and soul, with the freedom of those galloping horses that she no longer
feared Geta. She could stand near Melissa, and Melissa would not let him touch her again.

As she passed the Athena, she lifted both hands on
high.

"O Virgin Goddess, quick art thou to answer

prayer. Who but thou would answer prayer before the gift?"

So shriven and comforted, Chloé went back into the kitchen.

After this Chloé went no longer to the forest. She went every day to that break in the garden wall. She discovered a path, which she could reach from the hut and which led over a shoulder of the hill, all deep-forested, to the garden. Here she would come to watch the horse pasture. She learned the time of the morning ride, and she kept that appointment. No scolding and worrying of Melissa could dissuade her.

Sometimes she waited in vain for the precious sight. Sometimes the young Cornelius only came out, took horse, and rode away. Sometimes she saw only the Lady Verania and her daughters walking in the horse pasture. Then when Chloé went home she tried to walk sedately and slowly as they. In this she always failed. But her chief joy was the young Cornelius. She did not think of him as Roman—or as perhaps human at all. He was the beautiful and perfect rider. So Phaëthon had dashed onward with the chariot of the sun. So Hippolytus had ridden on the sea beach at the edge of the foam—that day when Arch Fear rose out of the sea and destroyed him. But nothing would destroy the young Cornelius. He had not a wicked, lying stepmother as Hippolytus had, but an own mother who constantly blessed him out of the air. Verania nearly always watched him ride away—and never, never did she omit that blessing out of the air.

Thus was begun for Chloé an imaginary but very real companionship. She pretended that she touched hands with these people, that she spoke to them and that they answered what she wished. She even accompanied them into their half-hidden villa. She even rode the horses, side by side with the god-like young man. She had lived all her life with imagined companions, the nymph of the wood, the Winds who came from Thrace, Notus and Æolus, trampling over the hut by night. These Cornelii were more real —her neighbors.

Sometimes as she watched from the wall, her imaginings would give place to bitter longing. She knew that, as a slave, she was as far away from them as a world. But for the most part she made them her own. Chloé was too old for such beliefs. Fourteen at this time. But she had had no contact with the world to make her less a child.

But in the autumn her Cornelii neighbors went away; and she saw them no more.

CHAPTER 13

Aulus Goes Home to Rome

Lo, that glorious Rome shall bound her Empire by
earth, her pride by heaven, and with a single city's wall
shall enclose her seven hills, blest in her brood of men.
                                                    Æneid, Book VI

Aulus Cornelius Maro was going home to Rome.
It was three years since he had left it. Three years
since he had left the mountain villa in Samnium
where he had ridden the horses to amuse his mother
and sisters. Three long years of soldier life in Spain,
and now he was going home. He was trying his best
not to get excited about it, but he was so happy that
every return of the thought sent through him the
quiver of a thrill. The best of it all, he was being
invited to come back, invited by the man he most
admired in the world. Tiberius Gracchus. Great Jupiter, what an honor!

Aulus had been with Gracchus in that miserable
affair at Numantia, when the Roman army under
Mancinus had been beaten by the Numantians and
driven from their camp. Further, the army had been
surrounded and likely to be annihilated. Tiberius as
quæstor had gone into the enemy's city, had treated
with the Numantians, and so saved thousands of Ro-

man citizens. But such a treaty was shameful to the Romans, and Tiberius had greatly feared its effect in Rome. He had been in despair, sure that his career was at an end. At an end! It was just beginning, as Aulus intensely believed and had earnestly assured him.

And now that assurance was being fulfilled. Tiberius had returned to Rome, leaving Aulus in Numantia. In the flare-up that greeted Tiberius, so many of the Romans had flocked to him, grateful to tears for the saving of their sons and brothers, that Tiberius had become the best-loved man in Rome. At the following election they made him tribune of the people, the most important office (in some ways) in Rome. Evidently this had but spurred him to further action. What was he doing now? Aulus could only guess, but he could guess pretty well.

When he and Tiberius had been marching with the army toward Numantia they had gone through Tuscany, and Tiberius had noted again and again that they passed no small Roman farms.

"Another big estate," Tiberius would say disgustedly as they filed slowly past, taking perhaps an hour to come to the end of the demesne. "Where are our small Roman farmers? Aulus, if we have no more farmers we will soon have no more Rome. Not a farm! Not a farm!"

Aulus had never forgotten the concern, the grief on his friend's face, the flash of anger when the army met in the road the gangs of barbarian slaves who had been made to take the place of honest freemen.

Even after they reached Numantia, the matter had been upon Tiberius's mind. He was brooding, brooding over this wrong to Rome.

"The rich men have taken all the land," he told Aulus, "while our landless farmers loaf in the streets of Rome, an army of Unemployed living off the dole. It is a wrong, an abominable wrong to the State."

Such brooding in the heart of a man like Tiberius Gracchus was sure to result in action. But what was he doing? The messenger had said, "Tiberius Gracchus wants you to come back to Rome. He needs every friend he can muster." Well, Aulus was his friend, and moreover his cousin. Aulus believed in his cousin with all his heart.

Who were Tiberius's enemies? Aulus did not know. He did not care. He was on Tiberius's side. He was on his toes ready to run to the splendid task of helping Tiberius, yes, and of helping the Roman State. Even in these late years of the Republic, Rome was in a sort the Roman's god.

It was two years since Tiberius had left the army and gone home. Two mortal years. And all that while Aulus, out in that god-forsaken country, Hispania, had fought when there were battles to fight, rested in camp when that was the order of the day, and finally under the general Scipio Africanus had helped to lay siege to the hill city of Numantia. That most trying, most debilitating business of *siege*. The very word is synonymous with boredom, day after day in the blazing sun, no fighting, no action, the soldiers growing sick and rebellious. Then had come

Tiberius's blessed messenger with his release, then the hurried journey on horseback to Valentia, and now the sea journeying. Everything had gone smoothly. In a few days they would be at Ostia. Aulus would take horse and gallop to Rome.

Every moment as he paced the small deck, some new phase of "home" came over him. First, most important, the Forum with its marble porticoes where now he would not be a mere youth but a full-grown man (Aulus was twenty) with a man's responsibilities for the Republic. How well he knew every turn and corner of the Forum, every precious tradition that belonged to it!

Then came his own ancestral house on the Palatine Hill which had belonged to the Cornelii for generations. He wondered if Drusus the porter would still be sitting at the door—dear old Drusus whom he used to tease so unmercifully. He hoped Drusus had not died or been replaced by a younger slave.

Aulus's father was still away in Gaul. The messenger had said so. Glory to the gods! There was no telling on which side his father would be. He might, as easily as not, oppose Tiberius's whole measure, and not only forbid Aulus to take part but range him on the other side. Horrible! Well, Publius Cornelius, his father, was in Gaul.

His father's severity, of the old-fashioned military sort, was almost unbearable to Aulus—unbearable and yet it must be borne. It was Roman law.

His mother! Ah, that was a different matter. At the thought of his mother Aulus's whole face changed. A sailor passing him on the deck stopped, thinking he was about to speak to him, so imminently expressive had the young Roman's face become. His mother! She was almost sure to approve Tiberius. She had always admired him and the younger brother, Caius. Also Tiberius's mother, the famous Cornelia, who as a widow had brought up the two boys and educated them; Cornelia was Mother's dearest friend. One would think they were blood relations instead of relations by marriage. His mother would be in the atrium reading a scroll Cornelia had loaned her, she would be at the door peering eagerly down the street because it was time to expect her son, she would be —well, wherever she was when Aulus arrived, how she would leap up to greet him. That expression of her face! Somehow it always said that since Gnæus, the older brother, had so disappointed her, she depended upon Aulus for all pride, all joy. Well, let her depend upon him, now he was having the chance to show what was in him.

His mind quickly leaped to another who expected much of him. Panætius the Greek philosopher who lectured in Rome, and had interpreted Stoicism to Aulus. And not only Stoicism but the ancient Epics of Greece. Gods—how the beauty of those old things sprang up when Panætius read them aloud! Aulus's whole mind had been formed and stamped by this man. Aulus was not alone in this. All the young men of Rome were so influenced by the Greeks. Some for good, many for ill. Whenever Aulus wanted mental refreshment it was to the Greeks he went for it. He read Greek as easily as Latin, spoke it as easily. He was a well-educated young man. When he was fifteen he had gone to Athens itself. Ah, those two years! Through all his life those would be his golden years.

"Look, look, sir," said the captain's respectful voice. "You must not miss that sight."

Aulus brought himself back with a jerk. The "sight" was indeed beautiful, a Roman trireme sweeping along on the whitecapped blue, its three banks of oars beating downward, upward, downward —for all the world like wings. Only an eagle's wings beat upon an invisible resistance; these with every downward stroke whipped the water into white foam. Its wake was white as snow—white and straight. "Good helmsman, that," said Aulus. Now as the trireme came nearer he could hear the flute of the oar-leader playing to keep time. It was an old tune his nurse used to sing to him. Who knows but that the tune may even yet be hummed in Italy, and no one knows its origin? Tunes have such life, clinging for centuries.

And now it filled Aulus's heart with the very essence of home.

As Aulus's ship had made its ten-day journey across from Spain, they had scarcely met another craft. But now for two days as they were nearing Rome the sea had been filled with vessels—merchantmen from the Euxine, or from the Ægean islands, bringing wine and oil, barges from Sidon crowded with barrels of oil, craft from Egypt bringing grain, and other ships from the mysterious coasts beyond the Pillars of Hercules where they found tin. The activity of all the world centering, drawing as toward a magnet—toward *Rome*.

"Tomorrow," said the captain, rubbing his hands, "if this wind holds we'll be in Ostia."

The wind indeed "held," and on the following morning Aulus landed at the port of Rome. He hurried ashore, took the horse which had been waiting there a week for him, greeted the hostler as though he were a brother; then, mounting, the slave attending on another horse, he set forth at a gallop. The road ran sometimes straight through open country, sometimes along the Tiber, an unbeautiful muddy river, especially here at its lower reaches, but to Aulus it looked the river of the blessed.

He reined his horse suddenly and began to go at a walk. He must control himself. Aulus took his Stoic philosophy very seriously. A Stoic must be unmoved by joy as well as by sorrow. The inference was that if you allowed joy to master you, grief would master you also. He walked his horse the rest of the way. But he could not "walk" his heart. That kept welling up with an emotion that brought tears into his eyes.

Now loomed before him the wall of Rome. He came to the Porta Trigemina. The gate was open, and, by Pollux, the porter remembered him and gave him a smile of good luck as he passed into the city. Eternal Rome! He was there at last. Everything looked strange, everything looked as familiar as an old shoe. He did not know which. He was in the valley Murcia where of old the Romans held games in honor of Consus, the god of Council. They had the Circus Maximus now for the games. How he loved the place and the races he had seen there as a boy, sitting on those wooden seats. For at this time the circus was entirely of wood. He was skirting the Palatine Hill, on the Via Nova. The whole road was filled with people going to market, for he had struck just the market hour. Good! The Forum would be filled. He turned into the Via Sacra. How familiar now was every house, every booth, every temple! How familiar! The crowds about him began to grow more respectable, better-dressed. Now he could hear the roar and gabble that came from the Forum. In a moment more—— Ah, he was there! The narrow street opened out into the sunny Forum space, color-ful, seething, the center of the world.

The Roman crowd was emotionally like our own. It performed with uncanny detail our actions, en-gaged in our occupations. Men here were bent on buying and selling mortgages, bonds, stocks; they were bent on lawsuits with "shyster" lawyers and with honest ones; they were seeking office, seeking jobs and not getting them. But externally the Roman crowd differed from ours in three respects: there were no machines, and no ladies, and, in mass, the crowd looked not black but white. It was not the dead white we picture on the stage but the beauti-

ful ivory white of natural wool. All togas were made
of it.

Aulus was delighted to see the togas. How grace-
fully the men wore them, old and young alike. He
wondered if he had forgotten. It took months—nay,
years—to learn to carry off the toga. It was the badge
of the Roman, the mark of dignity in all the climates
of the world. Great Jupiter, what a noise! Pandemo-
nium. He had forgotten the Forum roar out there in
Numantia. Aulus slowed his horse, allowing it to go
only step by step in the dense crowd. They were
about him like a close growth of underbrush. And
he didn't know a face—not a face.

Suddenly there was a clear, beautiful cry—the
most famous voice in Rome.

"Aulus—by the gods, it is Aulus Cornelius! Stop!
I'm coming to you."

And there, elbowing his way through the mass,
came Tiberius Gracchus himself, his splendid Roman face all alight with recognition.

He dragged Aulus off his horse, threw both arms
about him and kissed him.

How wonderful of him to do that before everybody! He was usually so dignified—even distant.
Aulus could hardly hear what he was saying, for
his own excitement and the buzz of the crowd.

"Good boy! How did you get here so soon? And,
by Pollux, in the very nick of time. I address the
people this morning from the rostrum. Most important. Come along."

"I cannot—I cannot. I am not even dressed. Look

at my dirty cloak. I haven't been home, haven't seen my mother."

"That's so. Well, hurry along and get back as quickly as you can. I'll hold it back for you if I can. I want you to understand fully, fully what we are doing."

He fairly lifted Aulus onto the horse again—gave the horse's flank a slap. Yes, he needed Aulus. There was no question of it, and he cared not who knew it, either. Proud as a king, Aulus took his way back to the Via Sacra, then up the steep to the Palatine Hill, toward his home.

The porter slave opened to him, almost cried with joy at seeing him.

Aulus hurried to the atrium.

"Mother!" he called. "Mother Verania!" She was not there. Then to her own room, to the further smaller atrium. She was in none of the familiar places. He went leaping up the stair to the large spinning room. And there he found her. She was standing by the brightest window, busy with her distaff. At sight of him she dropped thread and all, stretched both her arms wide and ran to him.

"My darling, darling Aulus!"

Yes, there was the joy he knew would be in her face, the pride—everything. Tears began to roll down his cheeks, and he did not care. He did not think of stern Stoicism or of anything else but that he was at home and in his mother's arms.

But in a moment he was stamping his feet as though he did not care for her at all; as if he only wished to get away from her. The affairs of the young are urgent, and of necessity the old are left out of them.

"Tiberius is making a speech. He says I must hear it. Important as the gods. Where is my toga? I'll only pretend a bath. Hurry, hurry!"

Of course his mother had everything ready. That was as certain as sunrise.

In an incredibly short time he was dressed, refreshed as youth is able instantly to refresh itself, looking like anything else that is joyous and in bloom. Yes, the toga folds stayed quite in place over his shoulder. He had not forgotten the trick. Hot and uncomfortable, though, a toga after life in the field. He was hurrying, striding toward the Forum.

So ardent, young, trusting Aulus Cornelius entered the fierce life of Rome.

CHAPTER 14

The Army of the Unemployed

He was too late! At least, when he entered the Forum, Tiberius Gracchus was in the midst of his speech and the crowd like a still pool below him. Aulus began elbowing his way nearer. Then he realized he could hear perfectly well from where he stood. What a voice Tiberius had! Clear, apparently not loud but reaching to the farthest edge of the square. How strange to hear that familiar voice in public speech! It had an emotional quality in its very tone, so that Tiberius needed not to force emotion into it. And the tempo of the speaking just right—much swifter than it seemed.

Every Roman loved oratory, from the wisest senator to the very slave boy in the street. But Tiberius apparently had no oratory, only his forceful reasoning in a diction always pure and carefully correct. He was standing now quiet in one spot, making few gestures, not disarranging his toga as some careless speakers did. His face was even gentle: but an earnestness flowed out of him and into the crowd. He had them completely in his power. Sometimes they stirred, muttered, then, for a long time, were still. Then like sudden thunder came their shouting—

shout after shout, so that Tiberius could scarce stop them to begin speaking again.

This is what he was saying:

"The savage beasts here in Italy have their dens, they have their places of repose and refuge; but you men who bear arms and expose your lives for the safety of Rome enjoy nothing more in this country than light and air. You have no houses, no settlements of your own, you wander from place to place, you and your wives and children.

"Isn't it rather amusing, my friends, my fellow soldiers, rather ridiculous, that your generals exhort you so grandly to fight for your altars, your sepulchers, when not one of you has a household altar for sacrifice, nor house of your own, nor hearth of an ancestor to defend? Oh, yes, you can fight, you can be killed; but it is not for this. Oh, no! It is to maintain the luxurious homes of the rich, the big estates of the landed owner.

"Where is your land, my friends? Where are your farms? What has become of the old laws of Rome that made these indissolubly yours—yours?"

Shouting drowned the voice, angry shouting now, shouting not to be denied.

"Put it to the vote!" yelled Aulus from his corner. And he started a whole section shouting that "Put it to the vote!"

A toga-clad senator lifted his hand. "Discussion," he called. "Are we to have no discussion? Why have we a Senate at all?"

"The vote, the vote!" insisted the crowd.

But in the end there was neither vote nor discussion. The opposing senators knew too well that in the present heat of the people it would mean defeat for them. All voting was put off to the next day.

By the end of the morning Aulus knew what Tiberius was doing. And he knew it to be about as dangerous as could be. Also it was as just as it was dangerous.

The common public land of Rome which the simple Roman farmers had farmed, and which they could by the old laws hold only in small parcels, had gradually in the last two generations gotten into the hands of speculators, rich men, and the aristocracy. At first, in secret, land had been added to land; but now openly (illegal though it was) financiers held these vast estates. The farmers, driven from the land by cheap slave labor, wandered the streets of the cities and of Rome, living off the dole.

What Gracchus proposed to do was to take this common land from its illegal owners, and allot it back to the farmers. He proposed to make once more a healthy state of Rome.

But would these rich men and rich senators give up their land so, for the health of the body politic? Indeed not! They were fighting the measure with all the strength and bitterness that was in them.

Aulus pushed through the crowd to the platform, joined Tiberius, and they walked home together.

"What a shame they did not vote," said Aulus. "The Senate is bound to let the law go through sooner or later. The people are yours—absolutely yours."

"Yes, I believe the law will succeed. It is not as if we were confiscating the land. It is to be paid for." Thus answered Tiberius, exhausted and a little dull after the mysterious effort of holding the vast Roman soul in the hollow of his own soul. Beads of perspiration stood on his forehead. He was longing to be at home and to get into his cool tunic. But he was only twenty-nine. His interest began to revive.

"It's a fight," he said. "A big fight. Marcus Octavius is the important man. You know of course, even if you are just come back from the wilds, that he is the other tribune with me. His vote will make or kill the bill."

"But Octavius? Hasn't he always been your friend?"

"Yes, and is still. But the biggest men of the senate are pulling and hauling at him night and day; saying the bill will overrule the Senate, give too much power to the people. He's loyal, though. Fine fellow—Octavius."

They turned a corner into their own street—walking in silence. It was a narrow street of wooden and rough-stone houses, windowless on the outside. Republican Rome was yet simple.

"Scipio sent his respects to Octavius by me," remarked Aulus innocently. (Scipio the younger was now general out in Numantia.)

"By Jupiter, he did!" exclaimed Tiberius, rousing yet more. "Don't fail to go today and call upon Octavius. Everything counts—every touch of friendship."

"Isn't today rather soon?"

"Yes, but go today."

They had reached Tiberius's house, just four doors from Aulus's. Families of the same *gens* lived in the same district.

"And come to dinner with me tonight," said Tiberius at parting. "I want you to meet my friends with all possible speed. Crassus will be there, Mucius Scævola, and Claudius Appius."

"By Hercules!" exclaimed Aulus. He walked onward, warm and excited, enjoying every turn of the affair. Crassus was Pontifex Maximus; Mucius Scævola, a famous lawyer, was this time Consul; Appius Claudius was a well-known Roman whose ancestor built the famous Appian Way.

"Why, with such friends as those he cannot possibly fail," thought Aulus.

It was yet early in the day. The Romans (like the Greeks) were early risers. In the summer they might be up even at four o'clock. Aulus was in time for the *cena* or old-fashioned midday dinner. His mother was waiting—hungrier to see him than for the meal. They had a happy time, sitting in cool, green shade of the awning in the atrium. She wanted to hear the whole of the morning's performances—she was eager to mingle with her son's interests.

"Cornelia trusts Tiberius without limit," Verania said. "She tells him she is sure he will be as great as his father Tiberius and as her father. She says soon she will not be called the daughter of Scipio, or the wife of Tiberius, but the mother of the Gracchi.

Caius, you know, is just as promising as Tiberius."

It was strange that the pronouncement of a mother should be so important in Rome. But Cornelia was no ordinary mother. No man in Rome had greater fortitude in facing grief, greater wisdom in facing joy. Her husband, Tiberius Gracchus the elder, had loved her so romantically that all Rome took note of it. She had borne her widowhood nobly—had refused the hand of Ptolemy, king of Egypt, choosing rather to remain faithful to her dead husband, and devoting herself to the education of the present Tiberius and Caius. So wise was she in her treatment of them that men considered she had done more for them than had their natural talents. Sayings of Cornelia have come down for two thousand years. It was she who, when young Tiberius and her younger son Caius came home one day from school, presented them to her rich, jewel-bedecked guest, saying, "These are my jewels."

Yes, all Rome loved Cornelia.

And Aulus had to tell his mother of his own adventures in Spain. Had he kept free of fever? Yes, entirely free. The battles? Had he been wounded? Yes. He had to show his scars to her, each one. And he did so, much as a little boy who comes in from play and shows his hurts to his mother. Her eyes shone with pride. "If I had only been there to nurse you," she said.

"Pooh, they were nothing," he answered. Romans were intensely proud of battle scars. Cato the philosopher is said to have had his breast entirely covered with them.

Verania in her turn told Aulus the news of home. His two little sisters were both married now and belonged to the jurisdiction of their husbands' *gentes.*

"It was so hard to part with them when they were still so young," said the mother. "But Lucia has a kind husband."

It might be guessed that poor little Paula had not. Paula was the younger. Aulus's elder brother, Gnæus, had been drinking again. He was running with a gay rich crowd and, though not rich himself, trying to keep up with them. He was ardently supporting a certain rich land-owning friend and thus was against Tiberius entirely. The opposing party was proud enough to get a Cornelius of good family into their ranks.

Aulus shook his head.

"Too bad, too bad," he commented. He noticed how tired Verania looked now, telling this.

"Well, Mother," he said gayly, "I won't get drunk. Great Juno, what a beastly, un-Roman thing to do! It's the Stoics who will sail the Roman ship, not the drunkards. Rome needs its best men now."

She laid her hand on his, a tender proud gesture.

"What did Father think?" he asked.

"Of Gnæus? Oh, they had a terrible quarrel just before your father left. Your father threatened to have all the relatives in, and *try* Gnæus by the law. I don't know what he would have pronounced. I suppose not banishment, nor public whipping, but——"

"Well, he deserved the whipping anyway," declared Aulus.

"Oh, no, no!" said Verania in such a trembling voice. It did not occur to Aulus that Gnæus had once been a baby in Verania's arms.

"Would Father quarrel with me if he were at home now?" he asked suddenly.

She looked steadily into his eyes.

"Yes, he would," she answered. "He is bitterly against this sort of reform. Not because of the money, but because it opposes the Senate. And the Senate is right always."

"Do you think that, too?"

She did not answer. In that silence Aulus might have read a whole lifetime of submission.

"Well," he said comfortingly, "he is not here, and he left no forbidding message. So I shall go straight ahead with Tiberius."

She took his hand, and he felt her press it nervously, as if she entered into his effort.

"I have had a letter," she said. "He will not be at home until spring. Perhaps by that time all will be settled." In a sudden flash, Aulus saw how thankful she was for the absence of the man whom she had obeyed since she was fourteen years old.

He put his arm about her.

"Never mind," he said. "If he comes home too soon, I'll try not to anger him."

"Oh, he could not come too soon," she said quickly, as though overtaken in a fault.

Aulus was so happy with his mother that they talked all through the siesta hour until it was time for him to go and call upon Marcus Octavius.

In after years Aulus was to treasure every moment of that home hour, every turn and gesture of the talk. He was to wish so regretfully that he had not gone away to Octavius, and that he had not spent the first evening away from home, at Tiberius's banquet.

But now the outside matters were all-absorbing, all-important.

CHAPTER 15

The Protagonist for a Nation

The call upon Octavius was entirely successful. The tribune of course knew exactly what the young man had come for, but he pretended not to know and he was genuinely glad to get the message from Scipio. Also he took a fancy to Aulus and accepted his invitation to dinner—for the night following the dinner of Tiberius.

How gay and forward-striding was the world!

On the way home Aulus met Publius Lævinus. He had almost forgotten Lævinus—the neighbor down the street. He had not thought of him once in all that time in Spain. But here he was again, familiar and friendly—"as though," thought Aulus, "you had gone off and left a garment hanging on a peg, and had come home to find it hanging there just the same." Lævinus was a friend of his father's and hence a part of Aulus's childhood. They greeted each other warmly, and Lævinus asked him the news of Numantia. Then they parted.

Lævinus, going home, snapped his fingers as though provoked at himself. Why hadn't he betrothed his daughter Lavinia to this younger son of Cornelius instead of to Gnæus? He had heard some rumor about

Gnæus that gave him pause. However, it was good to have a family alliance with the Cornelii. Gnæus would probably sober down. Lavinia was only ten years old as yet. In any case, it was beyond changing now.

Lævinus, by the way, did not feel the least like an old garment hanging on a peg. He had just been to the new public baths that had hot pools as well as cold. He felt particularly fit.

Aulus told his mother about meeting Lævinus. He had a cozy way of telling her such unimportant things.

"And you know," Verania told him. "Lævinus has betrothed his little daughter to Gnæus. Oh, I do hope Gnæus will be kind to her. Lavinia is such a timid little thing, and not very pretty."

"Has Lævinus ever been to his villa in Samnium?" asked Aulus.

"No," said Verania. "But I wish we could go to ours."

"We will," declared Aulus, "before Father comes home."

"Strange," thought Aulus, "that Lævinus never goes to his Samnian villa. It had to do with some old disgraceful love affair." Amusing to think of Lævinus in a love affair—when he was now so severe and dignified.

Aulus smiled and went singing softly to his room. The song he hummed was the rowing song he had heard on the trireme.

This was Aulus's last quiet day at home. After

that the days began to gather a strange, deep rhythm like a march to an unseen goal. Days of tensity and excitement and the low underground thunder of dread, days of triumph that clashed in his heart like cymbals. It seemed as though men made these events. Partly they did. But it was really a nation going over the brink. Rome, the Republic, would never be the same again.

The Rome to which Aulus had returned was a state startlingly like our own. That is, its problems were our problems. Not only were the people facing unemployment and dislodgment of the farmer, which Tiberius was trying earnestly to mend, they were facing internationalism. Rome's internationalism was created by her victories. These victories had hurt the conquered; but they hurt the conqueror yet more. Rome at this time had almost finished her world conquest. It was not our modern complete world. But it was all the world there was. Now Rome had to *live* with these foreigners just as we have to live with China, Japan, Europe, and South America. Fortunately we have not "conquered" these countries as Rome had done—in that we are better off. For now Rome had to wield the whole world, and she was not big enough to do it. Rome's best men were sent out to govern the provinces; her finest youth were sent out into the armies. For only by maintaining constant legions could she hold what she had filched. Aulus was an example of such exiles. Caius Gracchus, Tiberius's younger brother now in Numantia, was another; Scipio the younger, a third

(Plutarch complains bitterly of Scipio's absence at this crucial time). Lævinus had spent years in Egypt, Lævinus's father almost a lifetime in Spain. These men and more—from a single street in Rome.

Thus Rome was depleted. When the governors came home from ruling vast tracts as absolute monarchs, when the generals came home from ruling great armies, they found Rome small and inconsiderable. They were galled at obeying a company of doddering home bodies—the Senate. The Senate became afraid of her generals, and very much afraid of the returning armies. These armies and generals always claimed a "triumph,"—that is, a procession in which the trophies and loot from the conquered countries were displayed, and in which the pitiful captives were led in chains to tickle the pride of the populace. In the midst of such a "triumph" rode the general, clad in the splendor of shining armor and with a red cloak embroidered with gold. He was followed by pageants or floats showing the character of the countries he had secured for Rome. And at the end came the buffoon making jokes— for all the world like a modern clown. It was much like our circus parade. But it was a very dangerous circus parade, and the Senate was at this time beginning to avoid them. They would keep their prominent generals and prominent men *away* from Rome because they were afraid of their power over the people. The Senate would make complimentary appointments in foreign lands, or would flatly refuse consent to the return of such men. If they had real-

ized the powerful nature of Tiberius Gracchus, they
would have kept him away in Spain. Can one imagine
a folly so great? They did later keep away his
brother Caius. Caius had finally to return to Rome
without the consent of the Senate.

Rome's policy toward her provinces and her colo-
nies was equally foolish. She used them to enrich
herself. Rome did not deal unselfishly with her inter-
national problem. Unselfishness, insight into the rights
of others, was and is the only cure.

Today, in spite of diplomatic downfalls and cruel
armaments, the world seems slowly to be forced to
see the light. We seem to realize the new world-
neighborhood which has come upon us, and to feel it
with kindness and understanding.

We do not know. We can only hope.

But we know that Rome did not see. And now in
Tiberius's remedy for unemployment she saw nothing. In the splendid young Tiberius Gracchus himself, she saw nothing. She opposed him with all her
power.

In the Forum, on the third day after Aulus's return, Marcus Octavius voted against the land bill.
This was a great shock to Tiberius, and to the populace who had begun to look forward confidently to
receiving the land. Octavius had been so friendly, so
open to reason that Tiberius had had every hope
in the world of winning him. But the arguments of
august and respected men in the Senate had overruled

the young man's mind. Thus Octavius completely balked the bill.

Tiberius came home from the Forum looking broken as if with illness.

"I feel," he said to Aulus, "as though that law were the law of my life—that to kill it, kills also me."

"Perhaps if you wait," said Aulus with a wisdom beyond his years, "Octavius or the Senate will be obliged to change. They cannot forever refuse the people."

Tiberius's eyes burned. "I cannot wait," he said in sudden passion. "The people will never win without a leader. I am their leader. At night I seem to hear them calling to me to give them back their land."

It is sometimes given to a man to be protagonist for a nation. Tiberius knew with deep wisdom that the life of Rome was in this move. He was urged on by a national need, a surrounding atmosphere of longing, greater than the longing in his individual soul.

"Something must be done quickly," said Tiberius, "while the temper of the people is hot. I do not know what to do. But I almost know. I shall know by tomorrow morning."

The next morning Tiberius looked himself again. Buoyant and with a new resolve. He hurried to the Senate, and there proposed a new law—more drastic than the first. The land was to be confiscated at once, and the present holders were to receive no pay for what had been illegally gained.

The people went wild. It had just the effect of

enthusiasm which Tiberius had hoped for. But Octavius remained obdurate. The law was not put to the vote at once. Tiberius was too wise for that. He must persuade Octavius.

There now began a series of rival orations between Tiberius and Octavius which delighted the heart of Rome. Every morning in the Forum either one or both of them spoke. Every morning the people listened and grew more excited. Tiberius was the best orator in Rome, but Octavius was no mean antagonist. They spoke with drama, passion, intensity. "Yet," says the ancient chronicler, "though they spoke with utmost heat and determination, yet they never descended to personal reproaches, nor in this passion let slip any indecent expressions to derogate from one another." Marvelous young men! No wonder the populace loved them and came in greater and greater crowds. Argument of this sort was the very life of Rome. They loved it almost as they loved war.

But such argument only hardened Octavius's decision. Of course, after bringing so many reasons against the law he was the more convinced himself. The selfish land-owners stood behind him cheering him on. Octavius also owned a tract of the land. Tiberius now proposed to pay Octavius for the land out of his own (Tiberius's) money. As Tiberius had but a frugal fortune, this greatly touched the people. Octavius refused. It was again an impasse.

Tiberius had now come to a determination—a fanaticism, if you will, concerning the law. The bill had to go through. Obstacles in the way must be removed. After much thought, much hesitation, much fear even, Tiberius decided to depose Octavius from his tribuneship. This was as dangerous as could be. The tribuneship was a sacred office not to be dissolved by anything a tribune did. It was supposed that thus he could more freely serve the people. The tribune of the people must be inviolate. This was ancient law.

Not only would the Senate oppose. There was no telling what the superstitious people might think. Dignified senators of the opposing faction seized Tiberius's hands and in public besought him not to do so unprecedented an act. Tiberius had, however, a band of great public men (senators also) who approved and were willing to stand for him.

There followed one of the most sorrowful scenes— Tiberius and Octavius on the rostrum in the sight of all the people. Tiberius made the proposal, gave his reason, a truly good one, that if a tribune persistently voted against the people's wish he no longer represented the people and was no longer sacred. Then he pleaded with Octavius to avoid such needless disgrace. He seized Octavius's hands, his eyes filled with tears as he besought him to vote for the law.

"We two cannot agree. Put it to the vote of the people which of us they want. If they vote against me, I will go. If you, then you go. Why deprive these people of homes when they have suffered such hardships for Rome? Think what it means to be in need of a home, in need of a roof, in need of an altar to sacrifice to your ancestors!"

Octavius only shook his head.

Even now, so just was Tiberius that he did not rush the vote through that day. He adjourned the meeting. Next morning they met again—people, Senate, the two contestants. The crowd was restless, muttering. Again Tiberius pleaded. Octavius again refused.

Then Tiberius put it to the vote.

It was a slow, miserable business. They voted by tribes. Each tribe came forward and cast, man by man, the voting tablets into the large voting jars. Only the sound of the falling tablets broke the terrible silence. Then the counting. Then the announcement: "Octavius to be removed," and a hoarse shout from the tribe which had spoken. Octavius meanwhile stood before them, obdurate, pale as death. Thus voted thirty-five tribes. It needed only one tribe more to condemn Octavius. Tiberius lifted his hand, halted the voting. Then, weeping openly, he embraced Octavius with one latest bitter plea:

"Do not take this disgrace! Do not make me pass so odious a measure. Only speak and it need not be."

Octavius softened, his eyes filled with tears. He met Tiberius's look; he was on the verge of consent.

Then a hand waved to him from his group of proud friends who had pressed to the foot of the platform, the friends for whom he stood—their faces pleaded to him.

Octavius lifted his head, his look hardened.

"No," he said clearly. "My decision is the same."

Wildly the last tribe rushed forward. They cast their tablets, but these could not be heard for the shouts:

"Down with Octavius! Down with the land stealers. Down with Octavius!"

Dangerous men—men who had made war all their lives. They had killed at distance. They had killed hand to hand with their spears. Tiberius could scarcely quiet them to hear the last decision, announced from the rostrum:

"Octavius to be removed."

Then there was silence. Tiberius signed to some of his own men to lead Octavius from the platform. Perhaps he thought this safer. But when the men came to Octavius he resisted their touch. They had to grasp him and lead him down. This resistance, slight though it was, was enough to release the wolfish spirit of the crowd. With a howl they sprang to Octavius, pushing him, buffeting his face.

"Stop! Stop!" shouted Tiberius. He leaped from the platform, strove through the angry mass to Octavius's side.

"Do not touch him! Do not dare to touch him!" he cried.

Then Octavius, humiliated and disheveled, was led safely away.

So tragedy folded her mantle about this affair. She was not to lift it until the end.

CHAPTER 16

Dangerous Victory

At the next meeting Mucius, a client of Tiberius's, was elected tribune in Octavius's place. The new land bill was voted and passed. The thing was done! The Forum rang and rang again with the shouts of the delighted people.

Tiberius's triumph was complete. He could scarcely walk home for the rejoicing farmers who crowded into the narrow street, kissing his hands, weeping, calling him the savior of his people. The Romans were supposedly cold and emotionless, but under great joy or great hate they knew no bounds.

Cornelia met them at the door, her eyes wide and a little anxious. But the minute she saw Tiberius's face she knew that all was well. She folded him in her arms.

"At last!" she said. "At last!" She did not weep. She seemed too deeply stirred for that.

Aulus, standing with them, felt still dazed and unbelieving. Tiberius had wished for this since so many years. It seemed not possible that the hour was here.

As they entered the shadowy atrium, Tiberius said, "I feel as though an immense burden has fallen off me." Later he said, "I wish this had happened without the sorrow of Octavius."

"Do not speak of it," said Cornelia. "We must forget that now."

It was easy to forget the past in the glad business of the present. Three commissioners were appointed to survey the grounds and divide them equally. Claudius Appius, Caius Gracchus (Tiberius's younger brother), and Tiberius himself.

Caius was away in Numantia, so Aulus was appointed as his agent to act for him. It was happy, exciting work. Aulus had short sympathy for the wrathful owner who had to give up his villa estate when in many a case he had eight other villas to content him. But he entered wholly into the simple joy of the peasant who came in thankful wonder to the soil, so eager to build his little home. There would be acreage for perhaps a hundred such on a single estate. One peasant, by a strange chance, came into the acres that his ancestors had owned far back in the time of the kings. Surely the gods of Rome were on their side.

Out here in the sunny country one could hardly believe in the turmoil of Rome, even though the Senate peremptorily refused to let the land agents have a tent for their use, and allowed them only nine obols a day for expenses.

So a month passed.

But Rome was by no means quiet. It was seething like a pot which is just coming on to boil. The

fagots beneath burned as fiercely as ever. The Senate
hated Tiberius. Oh, how they hated him! Especially
Publius Nasica, who had held the largest tracts of
illegal land. He resisted the agents, had to be put out
by force. He made no secret in Rome of his hatred.
He and the other dispossessed land owners went
about the streets in mourning. They made a drama
of it.

The people of Rome on their side called Tiberius
their idol. They followed him in the streets, praising
him. The Senate hated such popularity and feared
it. When Aulus finished his part of the land work
and returned to Rome, he was amazed at the state
of things he found. Rumors flying like clouds in the
wind. Only that clouds are seen—these were secret
as sin.

An elder brother of Lævinus died. He had been
a strong advocate of Tiberius. The people immediately declared that the Senate had had him poisoned.
The body was burned, as was the custom in Rome,
but the people attended the burning in great crowds,
shouting that the very manner of the burning showed
the poison. It was almost a riot.

One night a slave of the household came to Aulus's
bedroom.

"There are two men out in the alley back of Tiberius's house," he said. "They are waiting to murder
Tiberius."

Aulus sprang out of bed at once. He summoned all
the men slaves of the home, gave them daggers and
two lighted torches, and went out into the black, dark

streets. As they came to the alley there was a sudden scatter of footsteps.

Aulus and his slaves gave chase, but the assassins were soon hid in the maze of old streets.

Almost immediately Tiberius arrived at his door. He was quite alone.

"You must not go alone again," said Aulus. And told him what had happened.

"I have known it for some time," answered Tiberius sadly. "I always go armed."

"To be armed is not enough. If you do not mind, I will go with you hereafter, and some of your own household should go as well."

The Senate, august and dignified, sitting in the Senate house, making the laws that have been models though all the centuries, was never in all its history above plotting in this manner—taking the life of the man who was inconvenient to it.

They were likewise working hard at another plot, one perhaps more reasonable, certainly more dangerous. They were trying to undermine Tiberius's popularity with the people. In this for a long time they had utterly failed. Tiberius was too single-minded, too honest and devoted to the people's cause for the Senate to make any headway against him. He lived frugally, caring not the least for pomp or show. He kept his promises. But now the plotters had a handle, a subject to work upon, namely the illegal deposing of Octavius. It was not a fair treatment of an opponent. Besides, the gods would punish such acts. The plotters tried to seize upon any slight misfortune as divine punishment, stirring up the superstition always so rife in Rome. Also, said they, why should a man work for the people as Tiberius worked? Surely only for one thing—to make himself *king*. Nobody was so unselfish as Tiberius pretended to be. Tiberius wanted to be king.

All these miserable rumors came daily to Tiberius's ears.

"But they will not so persuade the people," said the hopeful Aulus. "By the gods, if you could see those happy peasants on their farms! The whole state is filled with men who love you."

Tiberius shook his head. "They are easily frightened," he answered. "If a child dies of fever they think it is because Octavius was deposed. And then, too, they are badly off. They need stock for their farms. They need seed, everything—some of them are blaming me even now."

About this time King Attalus of Pergamum died and left great treasure of money to the Roman state. It was a god-given chance for Tiberius—both to reinstate himself with the people and to render actually effective what he had done for the Roman farms. He therefore proposed in the Senate that the moneys of Attalus be given to the farmers to restock their farms, that also the newly acquired cities of Pergamum be at the disposal of the people.

Pompeius, one of the senators, jumped to his feet.

"I am next-door neighbor of Tiberius, therefore I know what goes on. I happen to know that Endemus the Pergamenian came to see him. He presented

Tiberius with a purple robe because he is so soon to be King of Rome."

Upon this another senator sprang up, accusing Tiberius of feasting and rioting; a third recalled the deposing of Octavius. Tiberius denied these charges. Such confusion followed that the Senate had to be dismissed.

From this time onward Tiberius was on the defensive. They baited him in the Senate, questioning, heckling him until at times he became confused and could not answer. They kept up constantly the assertion that he wished to be king, and they harped day and night upon Tiberius's one illegal act, the deposing of his fellow tribune, Octavius. So little by little they were undermining the devotion of the people. Meanwhile, Tiberius's term of office as tribune was drawing to a close.

His friends, the men of power in Rome who had been with him from the first, now advised him to petition for the tribuneship the following year. The people still had enough trust in him to elect him.

To us at this far distance it seems as though Tiberius might have had wisdom to retire at this point. But he was young, vigorous, full of public vision. The reinstating of Rome upon her old democratic basis had become a passion in him. He saw the way to do it—and as in a trance he walked toward that goal. The opposition, the heckling, the dread of assassination had made him almost fanatical. Aulus, going with him to and from the Senate, to and from the marketplace, felt a strangeness in him. He was

silent, his face colorless. The moneys of Attalus were
not yet voted to the people. The Senate wanted that
treasure to dispose of among clients.

Tiberius became bold. He added to the Attalus
proposal others yet more radical and startling:
namely, a law to lessen the years of compulsory ser-
vice in war; another law granting liberty of appeal
from the judges to the people; yet another to join to
these senator-judges an equal number of the eques-
trian order.

These laws Plutarch tells us were too radical and
that Tiberius proposed them in an effort to win the
populace rather than for public good. They may have
been, however, part of a program which he had
hoped to complete. Now knowing that his time was
short, he set them forth all at once.

These proposed laws made a furor of hatred in the
Senate. And again the meeting was adjourned with
nothing accomplished.

Next day Tiberius went down to the marketplace
to plead with the people. The farmers had come in
with their produce, many of them the very ones for
whom he had secured homes and land. They greeted
him, but hardly with their old fervor. It was this
cooling of the people that was breaking Tiberius's
heart.

He spoke to them; it was a speech now famous,
in which he pleaded the rightness of his deposing
Octavius. Octavius had become no longer the repre-
sentative of the people. His tribuneship, however
sacred, was extinct. Did not the Romans deal so with

a Vestal virgin who had betrayed her trust?—and the Vestal virgin was most sacred of all. So he cited precedent—that so precious thing to Romans.

Aulus, listening—standing near—felt motions of dread in his heart. Tiberius was speaking with his old power—yes, and his old classic clearness—but there was under all he said an emotion of pleading, a terrible, tragic earnestness. Suddenly Tiberius changed—tears filled his eyes. He told the people plainly that his enemies had planned to break open his house that night and murder him. That plot, only an hour before, had been revealed to him.

Then the people broke into wild shouts of anger, shouts of devotion. Their love rekindled in a moment. They ran to him one and all, offering to guard him. Then they chose a group of their best to go home with Tiberius and guard his house. Aulus was put in command.

CHAPTER 17

The Outcome

That afternoon Aulus became alarmed about his mother. She had been ailing for weeks, fainting often at the slightest provocation. And now she was so weak that she had to keep to her bed. Truth to tell, she was suffering from some low nervous disorder brought on by the long years of anxiety to please and placate her husband, the recent years of worry over Gnæus and trying to keep his father from actually disgracing him, then the absence of her dearly beloved Aulus in Spain and in fighting, and now this strange gathering danger in Rome.

Aulus sat by her bedside holding her hand, speaking softly to her to make that sweet happiness come over her face—the look he loved so dear.

"Don't worry, Mother," he said. "Tomorrow the laws will be voted and all will be well. It seemed, before, that we could not win; but Tiberius triumphed, and he'll do it again."

"And you will be safe?" she pleaded. She was not public-minded like Cornelia. She loved her own, her dear ones she had brought into the world. And above all else, she loved Aulus.

Toward nightfall Aulus went out to take charge of

the guard about Tiberius's house. All night long he stood there. The men were armed, and they kept torches burning in the street. It seemed strange and sinister to have thus a military camp in the heart of Rome. Blossius of Cumæ came out of the house and stood with him. Blossius was a Stoic philosopher of great learning and had been Tiberius's friend and teacher for many years. When Blossius stood with him, Aulus felt somehow strengthened and hopeful. He kept himself alert to every danger and every possibility of danger. Gnæus had been for two weeks now living in the house of his rich friend, Tiberius's enemy. Aulus wondered if Gnæus was in any way connected with the plot of Tiberius's assassination. If so he would know every turn of Tiberius's house, every habit of his day. But Aulus was glad that Gnæus was absent. At least it kept his mother from realizing that her two sons were so bitterly opposed to each other. Every hour Aulus sent his slave to ask about his mother. The report was not encouraging. Aulus's heart grew heavy as the night wore on. Try as he might he could not quell the dread that clouded him.

At break of day came a soothsayer—whether a person sent by the plotters to frighten Tiberius, it is hard to say. He had a coop of chickens strapped to his back. This he set down in the street, opened the coop-door, and scattered grain to the fowls. Tiberius came to his doorway to watch. If the fowls came out and ate the grain, all would be well. If they refused, some misfortune was pending.

The soothsayer clucked and clucked with his tongue—not a chicken moved! At last one pullet ventured forth, fluttered its *left* wing, stretched its *left* leg, returned to the coop without pecking.

The men of the guard swore under their breath with fright. Aulus, weary with his night watching, shivered with cold. Even Tiberius bowed his head with infinite sadness. The soothsayer picked up his prophetic chickens, strapped the coop to his back again, and walked away.

It seems impossible that a man of Tiberius's learning and public foresight could have been afraid of such a nursery tale. But Romans one and all were superstitious—Greeks, too, for that matter, but Romans more. Lacking the Greek religious vision, that loving mood toward the Unseen, they resorted to auguries and signs. They must need perform the most exacting ritual in the world to keep their gods propitious. The whole Roman state was run by a series of lucky days which were somehow known only to experts. It is strange (or perhaps it is fitting) that the military conquerors of the world should have had a religion of fear.

Tiberius went into the house and arrayed himself, with that fine clean care peculiar to the Roman, in his white toga. Everyone knew that the meeting in the Senate was as serious as possible for the good or ill of Rome.

The new laws for the people would stand or fall today. No wonder Tiberius and all his friends felt breathless as they started out.

They had not gone far when two ravens were seen wrangling on a housetop on the *left* side of the street. The ravens (most ill-omened of all the tribes of birds) dislodged a stone which fell at Tiberius's feet.

"Do not go!" cried out one of the party. "No, no, Tiberius, do not go!" pleaded another, holding him by the arm. "The gods have spoken. They could not speak plainer than this." Aulus kept silent, not knowing what to say.

Tiberius stopped. He was utterly disheartened by all these miserable signs. Hope was not so rampant within him in any case.

"Perhaps we will wait," he said.

Just then a messenger came running.

"Your friends are ready," he told him. "They have come out in a splendid crowd and are calling for you."

The Greek philosopher Blossius spoke to encourage him.

"Surely, Tiberius, it would be a shame for the protector of the Roman people, the grandson of Scipio Africanus, to stop for fear of a silly bird."

Tiberius laughed at that. The spell broken, they went onward toward the Forum and the Capitol. And surely he was glad he had done so. At the first glimpse of him the people went wild with joy. They clamored and shouted. And as Tiberius advanced to his usual place, the friends came in a body about him so that no dangerous persons could get near him. Nearest of all was Aulus. So they mounted the rostrum. The Senate had met in the Capitol. The people were to vote here in the Forum.

Now Mucius, the fellow tribune with Tiberius, proposed the law concerning the treasure of Attalus. Immediately such a deafening clamor, such pushing and confusion arose below in the crowd of voters that no voting could be done. If Tiberius's friends were strong, so also were his enemies. Now Flavius Flaccus, a senator-friend of Tiberius's, came down from the Capitol and began to elbow his way through the crowd. It was with the greatest difficulty that he reached Tiberius at last.

"Tiberius,"—he spoke loud amid the din—"the rich senators have formed a conspiracy against you. They have come armed to the Senate, they have servants armed. They are planning to kill you *here* this morning."

The mad crowd had fixed its attention upon Flaccus. They knew something important was being reported. From the far edge of the crowd certain friends of Tiberius's called anxiously:

"What is it? What is it? What is Flaccus saying?"

Tiberius could not possibly make his voice reach to them. He motioned to his head, trying to tell them of his danger.

Immediately some clever enemy yelled:

"Tiberius asks for the crown. Tiberius is asking for the crown."

The crowd took it up. It became an ocean roar.

"Quick, quick!" cried Aulus, seizing a halbert from

one of the officers. "We must arm ourselves against the conspirators. Quick, quick!"

Upon this, other friends seized the halberts from the guards. They tucked their togas into their belts so as to be free to fight. They stood about Tiberius.

But now already they saw the conspirators themselves, the senators led by Nasica, the arch enemy. They had charged down the steps from the Capitol and were now forcing themselves through the crowd. The people, fearing these most august men of Rome, fell away as they pushed them. On, on they came. They reached the rostrum steps.

Suddenly the fighting commenced. Wild confusion, blows, yells—fighting that was so close that friend hit friend in the mêlée. The senators felled with clubs and swords. Tiberius's men fought with what they had. But spite of their defense the conspirators mounted the steps. Ah, they had reached the platform! They were no longer men but wild wolves.

Aulus had put himself directly in front of Tiberius. He was fresh from the war, skilled in fight, quick as a cat. Right and left went his blows.

One man after another went down beneath him. He was keeping Tiberius safe, safe!

Then sudden blackness——

Aulus fell backward in the press. Some enemy lifted his body above the heads of the crowd and threw it down the steps to be out of the way. Now Tiberius!

But Aulus had given Tiberius time to flee. Friends fled with him off the back of the rostrum, onward, chased by the maddened men. Tiberius received a blow on the head. He stumbled. He tried to rise. Then Publius Satureius, a proud senator, hit him, then Lucius Rufus. Then a dozen men. Tiberius was dead long before they stopped. But the crowd, mad, with no more purpose than wild wolves or tigers, surged onward toward the river, killing everywhere.

Thus died Tiberius Gracchus, the most devoted statesman that Rome ever had.

Aulus in the mêlée had been kicked underneath the platform. There he lay in the shadow unseen. Unseen? There was no one to see him; for the littered Forum was as deserted as an open field. Hours passed. He came to, at last, and crawled farther under the hiding. He had not been badly hurt, only stunned by the blow on his head—a miraculous escape. But what was the use of escaping? Tiberius was dead! He had failed to save him. What was the use of being alive!

In the late afternoon, through sheer boredom Aulus crawled out. What a littered Forum, torn garments, fragments of wooden stools which had been broken up for weapons, dead bodies! The Forum! Center of the Roman world—of Roman law! How horrible!

But now in the fresh air and on his feet, Aulus thought of his mother. Of course he must go to protect her—go at once. He walked, staggering, toward the Palatine.

Tiberius was dead. He had failed to save him.

Tiberius, Tiberius! Aulus's mind was so filled with this that he did not see where he walked. He found his street by blind habit. Because he did not care whether he lived or died, no one molested him. Indeed, he met no one. The streets were as empty as though in a city of the dead. Far away he could hear the shouts of the rioters; but here on the Palatine all was still. Rome was a city of fear.

He came to his home, opened the door. Absolute solitude and silence.

"Mother, Mother!" he called wildly.

He ran to her room. There was her bed, tossed as though she had fled in haste. He ran to the kitchen. Out from a closet peered the face of a little scullery maid. But she hid her face, screaming:

"You are dead. You are dead, master."

"I am not dead," said Aulus, shaking her roughly. "Where is everybody? Where is your mistress?"

"They ran away to Lævinus's house. Oh, master, take me with you."

"Come if you want," answered Aulus. But he was out in the street before the completed sentence, the slave girl running with him.

Yes, Lævinus had kept aloof from this business. His house would be the safest. But Lævinus was away now in Ostia. He could not help.

The door was barred. Aulus pounded on it, calling. His own porter peeped from the upper window.

"It's the master! The master!" he screamed. He ran down, flung open the door, and threw both arms about Aulus in delight and love.

After the bitterness of this day, even a slave's love was sweet.

"The messenger told us you were killed," the porter told him.

"How is your mistress?" demanded Aulus.

"Ai, she'll be better now she knows you're living," said the man. "Come this way."

He led the way to an upstairs room, where all the family had gathered. Verania was there, lying on a bed.

What a meeting! Aulus, stepping into the room so suddenly, unannounced, whole and alive.

"Aulus, my darling—oh, thank the gods!" cried Verania. She sprang out of bed, ran across the room to him, and fainted in his arms.

He carried her to the bed again, laid her gently upon it. Then he saw her face! Young as he was, Aulus had seen death too often in battle not to know it now.

"Oh, help me! Somebody help me!" he cried.

Immediately Cornelia was at his side. Together they tried to give the remedies the Romans knew. But Verania responded to nothing—quite gone, white and still, and, in spite of their bestirrings, at peace.

"It is no use," said Cornelia softly. "She is gone."

Then Aulus threw himself upon the body, sobbing aloud, calling his mother's name, kissing her hands.

"I have killed you, the only one left to me. Tiberius is gone, and now you. I have killed you, Verania."

The terrible strain of the day had broken him

completely. Cornelia put her hand on his shoulder. How calm she was in spite of her own profound sorrow!

"Do not say such things. You came to your mother in love. You did not kill her."

"But if I had waited——"

"No, it would have done no good. My boy, I have seen this coming since yesterday."

He was kneeling by the bed, holding his mother's hand. He tried to control his emotion, but it swept him again. The Roman, when once his calm broke, was in a very wildness of storm. Now his love beat backward toward Tiberius.

"Tiberius is dead. I tried to save him and I failed —failed. Oh, why is it not I in his stead? Tiberius was the life of Rome."

"Hush, hush," said Cornelia pityingly.

"But I ought to have saved him," Aulus insisted childishly. "I dealt with some of them. Then came a blackness. I think they hit me on the head."

"They did indeed," said Cornelia. "There is a welt as big as an egg, and it has been bleeding." She touched his forehead.

"It is nothing, nothing. I should not have minded it. Why couldn't I stay fighting? It was no time to fall into a heap. I failed."

"Listen to what I say," commanded Cornelia. "They told me—those who brought the news—that you fought desperately for my son, that you were his best defender, you do not know what you did."

"Nothing is of any account unless I could save

him," asserted Aulus who, as a Roman soldier, was accustomed to put through what he attempted.

The room began to darken with twilight.

Helvia, Lævinus's wife, now came with slaves bearing water to prepare Verania's body for burial. She was neighborly and kind. Her children were still in the room. Lavinia weeping bitterly for Verania, whom she loved and to whom she had looked for protection when she must marry Gnæus. Kæso, the son, a strong, sensitive boy newly grown tall, kept his eyes, dark and lustrous, fixed upon Aulus because he had so lately come from battle.

Now Cornelia led them all out. The children she bade go into the next room with the porter-slave, but Aulus she took down to the dim atrium. She could not help loving this youth who had loved her son so dearly.

"Aulus," she said earnestly, "of course you know that you must escape from Rome. Your life here is not worth a straw. They are killing all of Tiberius's followers and may break in here upon you at any moment."

"No kind of death can keep me from burying my mother," Aulus answered flatly.

Cornelia knew he would say this. No self-respecting Roman would say otherwise. To perform funeral rites was a solemn religious duty—the most solemn of all. They were called *iusta facere*—doing justice to the dead. All the happiness of the departed spirit was supposed to depend upon them.

"Yes, and that is right," said Cornelia as if reasoning with a child. "But I will perform them, and I know absolutely what is due." Other families in Rome burned their dead, but the Cornelii alone buried theirs according to customs especially sacred. Cornelia would be wise in these customs.

"Besides," she said, "Gnæus, whatever his faults, will not neglect his mother's burial."

"Gnæus shall not be alone in honoring my mother," answered Aulus.

Cornelia went on: "Yet you would want to fulfill the very last wish she had for you, would you not?"

Aulus nodded.

"Today Verania and I had a plan together. It was her plan first; I only joined her in it. We procured two horses, one for you and one for Tiberius."

Suddenly Cornelia's calmness left her. She bowed her head, utterly unable to speak. Her shoulders shook. Aulus laid his hand upon her arm. He dared not do more. There was that about Cornelia which forbade it. She stood so for several moments. Then she lifted her head and went on:

"Verania wanted you both, in case of trouble, to flee to your villa in Samnium. It is so remote and little known. We sent my slave Duro—you know him, the most trusted one I have—to be with the horses, at the Porta Esquilina. Even though Duro hears that —Tiberius is dead—he will stand there until I release him. He is so trained."

Aulus stood silent, still unconvinced.

"Oh, my dear Aulus, if you could have seen how your mother used her very last strength in making this plan—all the details, the package of food prepared with what you especially eat—Duro has it."

Aulus still stood silent. But Cornelia saw she had won. People usually did what Cornelia wished them to do, her fairness and judgment were so clear. But Aulus insisted on certain things. Dangerous though it was for him to be in the street and in his house, he accompanied his mother's body to the atrium of their home, saw it properly laid upon the bier with feet to the door. Then he scattered upon the body three handfuls of dust. This was ceremonial burial. Even if Cornelia should utterly fail in her promise (an outcome most unlikely), this would lay his mother's spirit, so it would not wander at night weeping through the house. Then Cornelia took from the family altar his bulla, the charm he had worn in childhood and, because it was a time of extreme danger, put it again on his neck. Then Aulus gave one long, long look upon his mother's face. He was ready. Cornelia brought a slave's tunic and a cloak, a sword and a dagger.

"These, also, Verania prepared for you," she whispered. "And this tablet is for Duro, with my command written upon it."

She went with him to the back door of the house, opened it, peered out anxiously. Then she kissed Aulus and shut him out into the world. The streets were black as pitch.

Aulus had played in these streets. He knew every turn and corner of them. He felt his way out of the alley and along the house walls, passing carefully the

Hermæ which stood as divine guardians at the doors. Not a soul was abroad. But from afar confused sounds and screams told him that the rioting was still going on.

Three hundred of Tiberius's friends were killed that night and their bodies thrown into the river.

Suddenly, just beyond him, a door was thrown open and a rout of men poured forth. Their flares lit up the street. Aulus instantly darted down an alley. If they had seen him he was gone. But they did not see him. They ran drunkenly onward toward the far-off confusion.

Aulus crept out again. The flares had indicated the way. He found a rude path leading down the back of the Palatine Hill, then along the valley at the foot of Esquiline. Here even in the dark he knew where he was because of the terrible smell of dumps and the open grave pits on the Esquiline Hill. The bodies of poor slaves and animals were cast here without burial. No wonder Rome was sometimes visited by epidemics which carried away whole families.

Now Aulus skirted along the high Servian Wall— the ancient wall of Rome toward the Porta Esquilina. Oh, why had he not realized it before! The Senate would guard every gate of the city to keep Tiberius's party from escape. Aulus went sick all over. Now that he was in action he wanted intensely to live, intensely to win free. He crept stealing nearer. Peered around a bastion. Yes, there it was—the Esquiline Gate. A torch burned in the ponderous archway. The flickering light shot up and revealed the great stone towers of the gate fortress. The gate was of course closed for the night. He stood still as death. If he called for Duro, the Senate's guard might rush forth and seize him. If he kept still he would certainly be caught at dawn. He decided to take the chance. He stepped boldly out and knocked at the porter's door. Instantly came a voice from an upper window:

"Who goes there?"

"I want Duro. Where is Duro?" demanded Aulus.

"Duro's gone. Who are you, anyway?"

So far the place kept perfectly unmoved and still. Aulus tingled all over with the expectation of sudden seizure.

"I am sent from Cornelia with a message for Duro," he called.

"How do I know you have a message?"

"I have a writing."

"Send it up."

A basket was lowered. Should he part with Cornelia's precious tablet? He decided to do so.

He had to wait a long time while the man brought a torch from within. Then he heard a grunt of satisfaction from the porter. Then the clank of mail as the man descended the stair. Would the Senate's guard be with him when he opened? But no, the porter stood alone.

"Duro went off," he said gruffly. "Tiberius was dead. What was the use to wait for him?"

"Let me out nevertheless," commanded Aulus. "And give me back my tablet."

The man returned the tablet to his hand. Slowly

the great brass-bound doors opened, a crack only. But Aulus was out like a flash—into the great silent open field. He began to walk swiftly along the paved highway—the Via Tiburtina. He came to a wooden bridge over the Anio River. Suddenly he heard footsteps behind him. He faced about, sweeping out his sword.

"Don't thrust me, master," came a voice. "It's Duro. I heard you call." (Great gods, how sweet it was to hear a voice he knew.)

"I have the horses yonder tied to a post. Oh, please, master, don't tell Cornelia I came outside the gate."

"I'll probably never see Cornelia again," said Aulus bitterly. "Hurry! Where are the horses?"

They stumbled over the rough ground; found the animals.

"Give me the best one," said Aulus, and was on its back with a single leap.

"Here, master, is the food." Duro thrust the package into his hand. Aulus suddenly realized that it was this last gift of love from his mother which had made him come. He clattered away, regained the highway, and urged the horse to a gallop. He must put as many stadia as possible between himself and Rome while the night lasted. He would surely reach the town of Tibur before dawn. Then he must push on to Varia, where an obscure path led along the Anio River up into the mountains.

Before he reached Tibur, rain began. Aulus drew his cloak up over his head and pushed on.

How happily he had come home to Rome! How full of joy and well-wishing! And now, a huddled, hunted figure, he fled from the city he loved, with no hope, no desire to return.

CHAPTER 18

The Stag and the Hunters

Aulus arrived at the Villa Cornelia after night-fall of the second day. The place which on former visits had been so full of lights and laughter was now dark and silent, as were his beloved dead. The rain of the lowlands here had turned to snow. There was a glimmer of light from the kitchen. Thither he went and found the eight slaves (all that were kept there in the winter) gathered around the fire.

They sprang up as if they had seen a ghost. Aulus told them he had come to get well of a sickness. The fiction needed no backing, for Aulus looked as they had never seen him—haggard and white. They scurried about. One ran out to care for the horse, another built up the fire to a roar. Olipor, the vilicus, brought him food. Fortunately Olipor was a man whom Aulus could trust. In his bedroom Aulus told Olipor the truth, and that his return to the villa must be kept as secret as possible. Then Aulus went to sleep almost before he had ceased talking, and slept for the greater part of two days.

He awoke rested but unrefreshed, sorry that the exhaustion had dispersed and left his thoughts clear. For now his mind leaped as if upon swords from

one sorrow to another. The two persons he loved—
the only two in the world—were dead. The city
which was to him godhead and home was in the
hands of enemies. His career at the age of twenty
seemed completely closed.

One wonders how people of the ancient world
met their griefs. These griefs were of more cruel
nature than ours, and the people had, so it seems,
less spiritual weapons to meet them. That they did
meet them and bear them in all those deep and
long-lost centuries is a keen comment on the in-
trinsic worth of men. Primitive man had a persistent
unbelief in death. The continual renewing of the
race sprang up in his heart as immortality and life.
Again and again in legend and springtime festival he
renewed his heart. But Aulus was not a "primitive
man"—far from it! He lived in a sophisticated age,
an age of disillusionment when the old simple *nu-
mina* (the unseen powers of hearth and field) had
"gone dead" from Roman minds. The aristocratic
society of Rome, in table conversation, in their fashion-
able plays, laughed at the old gods, were vastly
amused at the amours of Jupiter, and the two-head-
edness of Janus. Yes, the old gods were gone and
there was naught to take their place save philosophy.
Aulus had that in plenty. His master Panætius was
no common man, but a Greek philosopher of high
character and genius. Would his Stoic teaching serve
Aulus now?

As a Roman, two courses were open to Aulus—
the first was suicide. This did tempt him not a little.

Verania, his mother, was dead; Tiberius, his hero friend, was dead. Aulus was not at all sure that they still existed. Perhaps in the vague way of general existence beyond the Styx they wandered forlorn. Why not make an end and follow them? There was no one in the present world to care. He might have a chance of meeting them—there beyond the Styx. His self-destruction would be a mark of his love for them. They would approve it. It was a thoroughly Roman thing to do.

The other course was to face grief with philosophy —that Stoic philosophy, a gift of Asian Greece, which the Roman mind seized and made its own. The very name has become a synonym for the hard, tearless endurance of the shafts of fortune.

Aulus thought little now of danger. He should perhaps have stayed in the house to keep himself unseen; but in his present mental suffering this was impossible. Let the neighbors see him and report to Rome. Let the agents of the Senate come down and murder him if they wished. It would save Aulus the trouble. At any rate, he was not going to make an abject prisoner of himself.

The house, the atrium, the porticoes, so full of his mother's presence, were more than he could bear. He wrapped himself in the warmest cloak he could find and went out to stride the muddy roads, or to ride madly on his sturdy little gallic pony—coming home at night covered with mud, or wet to the skin with snow or rain.

About a month after his arrival came the secret

message from Cornelia that he had been banished "by name" from Rome—he and all Tiberius's followers. This dropped the last stone into the heaviness of his heart. That night he came the nearest to suicide as the way out. The cruel demolishing of himself was not so difficult for Aulus, who had fought in battle hand to hand, sword against sword, close up with living men. Bion, the vilicus of Lævinus's villa, had brought the word in one of his necessary journeys. With it he had Cornelia's message written on a tablet in her clear Latin printing:

"Do not despair. There will yet be work for you to do."

This saved him. After all, Cornelia spoke from the midst of the same sorrow that was his. Perhaps a worse sorrow. Would he let a woman outdo him in endurance?

So that morning, as he tramped the frozen roads, Aulus started to find that endurance. A Stoic saying crossed his mind:

"To the truly wise man no misfortune can come."

Well, then, he was not truly wise. For misfortune had surely befallen him. He would grieve over the death of Verania and Tiberius as long as he lived. But even this thought he tried to quench in the effort he was now making.

Aulus was for the first time facing the Unseen. This was difficult enough for a Roman. For they were the most practical and this-worldly of all the races of history. He began to recall the sayings of Panætius, so changed now as they presented them-

selves to his mind when the need meant life or
death, so different from the pleasant schoolroom sayings in Rome.

There were no more gods. There was only the
vast Reason which controlled the universe. Aulus as
a man took part in that Reason, *was* part of it. He
must remake his life according to Reason. Aulus did
not dwell on this as a matter of pure thought. He
(being Roman) began at once to put it into practice,
in that remarkable fashion which is almost difficult
for us to believe.

Some Romans took life as one vast indulgence in
all the sensualities they could lay hold of. Their
number was daily increasing in Rome. Others, of
whom Aulus was a type, held themselves to an ideal
with unrelenting purpose. These were they who held
Rome together in spite of the Indulgers for five
hundred years to come. To keep himself pure in body,
pure in action; to practise virtue as an athletic, ex-
ercising the soul exactly as if it were another body,
to keep his self-respect at high-water mark and never
do anything to offend it—all this Aulus now began
to do.

Because it was cold, he went without his cloak.
He ate only frugally. He would not allow himself to
think of his grief, or even of his anger against the
plotters in the Senate. He would walk all day in
rain or snow and, denying that he was tired, take
a rush-light and begin to read. Or if he allowed himself an early sleep he would have Olipor waken him

and begin to read again. Such it was to be a Roman Stoic in the second century before Christ.

Now it happened that he had at the villa only one book of philosophy—the Paradoxes of Zeno. For the rest there were a few scrolls he had brought from Athens, Homer, several books of Plato, and some plays of Euripides. Reading these, Aulus was refreshed beyond his planning. The beautiful, strengthful, *unreasonable* poetry would follow him on the road as he walked. Often when he had intended to think of Zeno's maxims, the pure loveliness of some Greek line would "sing" the maxim away. Being stronger in rhythm and deeper in meaning, the poetry would gain the day in his mind. No Roman could make such poetry—nor did ever make it—but he could be so deeply moved by it that it changed the whole Roman mind. So now it possessed Aulus's mind and heart. It made him wistful where he wished to be serene.

It was about this time that the people at the Villa Caracinia became aware of Aulus's presence. Instead of "people" at the villa, one should really say "Robina." Bion had known of Aulus all through the winter and had secretly brought him messages and even money from Rome. The shepherds had seen him frequently on the hills and had thought no more of it. But when Robina saw him one day down in the pasture he at once became news. She came running out of the kitchen one sunny morning and into the long shed near the storeroom. There Melissa and Chloé had come to get their week's supply of wool.

"Great Baal, what do you think now!" she exclaimed. "The young master Cornelius is come back to the villa over yonder. He goes about all alone, not even a slave with him. They say he must have committed some crime and had to run away. And they say——" She gave out of breath but had to finish her news. "They say that dreadful things have been happening in Rome. I don't know what. Geta heard about it in Aufidena."

Chloé set down her basket of wool.

"Wait a moment, Melissa," she said. "I must go and see."

She ran off before Melissa could object.

Melissa did object.

"Chloé is getting the very manners of a slave," she pondered, "running to spy upon what people are doing."

Chloé ran to the garden gate and into the garden —past the overgrown hedges of box, and the calm sweet statue of Athena where she usually paused for a moment, straight to the broken wall at the edge of the hill. He was come back—Hippolytus—Phaëton —the hero of all heroes in her mind.

There, below, was the horse pasture, very wet with the rains and delicately green with spring. A horse was standing bridled and waiting and the slave with it.

"He has come back, he has come back," her mind was singing. How wonderful if she should see him again after all these years! She had thought he would never, never return. He must come out in a moment;

his horse was ready. She waited and waited. To see the young Cornelius would be such a refreshment, like a visit to Aufidena; or even Sulmona on a market day. Chloé was so tired of the farm with its monotony. She had never been away from the farm. Never seen even the little, littlest village. She had never seen the sea. That was the greatest sight of all—blue as if the sky were come down to earth and very smooth if there was no wind to ruffle it. *"Thalassa,"* she said under her breath—the Æolic word for "sea."

Melissa was calling. Chloé ran obediently to the gate. She had never disobeyed Melissa. The very necessities of the slave labor compelled her to obey. But now she resisted.

"Wait for me—just a while longer. It won't be long. He is sure to come."

But Chloé had already returned to her vantage point. And at that moment—the very luck of the gods!—Cornelius came out, walking slowly, with no eagerness at all. He spoke to the groom, who led the horse away. Then Cornelius walked across the pasture into the house again, a severe, slow, meditative gait and with bent head. Such a change! What had happened to him? No longer the bright, quick creature she had loved to watch. No longer a boy—but a dignified man of whom she would be afraid.

Chloé was troubled. She had made a mental fiction about Aulus without knowing it. Now that fiction was awry. His present conduct did not fit it. She

hurried back to Melissa, and they started home-
ward together.

"Why did you spy upon the young Roman?" asked
Melissa crossly. "Especially when Robina says he has
been guilty of crime."

"He is not guilty," asserted Chloé.

"My child, you know nothing whatever about it,"
returned Melissa.

"Well, neither does Robina. She just says what
comes into her head."

"That may be. But at least you have no right to
say he has done nothing amiss when he has come
down here so secretly. And Robina says he is quite
changed."

"I do not know why he came; but he is not guilty
because—because——"

"Because he is young and good-looking," finished
Melissa. "I am ashamed of you, Chloé."

In the midst of this quarrel Bion met them and
turned to walk with them. Bion had just come back
from Rome.

"What is all the argument about?" he inquired.

Chloé began eagerly:

"Oh, Bion, do you know what is the matter with
the young master, Cornelius? It isn't true that he
committed a crime. It can't be true."

Bion looked grave.

"Are they saying that among the people? That is
dangerous—very dangerous for the young man. He
is fleeing from Rome. In fact, he is banished. But it
is for a particularly decent deed, defending his friend

Tiberius Gracchus. Cornelius has been down here for months. We have managed to keep it secret. It isn't impossible that the plotters against Gracchus would send men down here to kill him."

"Oh!" breathed the fascinated Chloé. This not only fitted in with her pictures of Aulus. It made them better.

"Tell us more—more!"

"Can I trust you, Chloé, to keep still about it? You do not look as if you would."

"Oh, yes, yes."

So Bion told them the whole tragic story. Farmer that he was, his sympathies were deeply engaged. As for his hearers, they listened breathless. No tale of Iliad or Odyssey was as wonderful as this adventure so near home. Melissa listened almost as eagerly as Chloé. She too was famished for news, action, anything to break the dullness of the long hours of work.

The three were halfway up the hill before Bion finished. Suddenly there was a crashing sound in the bushes. A wild stag appeared, high-antlered, his pitiful eyes rolling with fear. He was running straight for them. Seeing them, he gave a snort of terror, wheeled, and like a curving star went leaping in great slow saults above the underbrush.

"The hunters are after him," said Bion.

"Oh, I hope—I hope they won't get him!" cried Chloé. To her the hunted creature was a very symbol of the hunted Cornelius, driven from his home and pursued by cruel men.

A moment later the disappointed shepherds came clambering and shouting up the hill.

"Why don't you set a trap for him?" called out Bion. "You'll never get him now. He's far away by this time."

"Oh, may Artemis protect him!" exclaimed Chloé piously.

"Artemis does not protect the stag," laughed Bion, full of the pleasure of the chase. "Artemis herself hunts the stag and the boar."

"But sometimes she protects them," insisted Chloé, "if they are young and have never been chased before. His antlers were all soft with velvet."

She seemed herself to feel the wild heart of the stag beating so furiously as he urged himself to leap onward. Her whole instinct was closer to the woodland thing than to the men who chased it. She knew the woodland creatures heart to heart, mind to mind. She did not know people.

CHAPTER 19

"Like the Sudden Night"

The next day after this there happened to Aulus something so cruel, so unwarranted and "chancy" that at first he could only throw away his god of Reason and cry out against confusion and stupidity.

Yesterday he had received through Bion a message from Cornelia, the first glimmer of betterment for him. The tide was turning in Rome (so the letter told). The senator, Nasica, who had headed the conspiracy against Tiberius, was now so hated that men gibed at him in the streets. The Senate had to give him an office in Africa to get him safely away from the city. Also the Senate had never dared to revoke the land law. Tiberius dead had yet accomplished his wish. Aulus's heart swelled with pride for his friend. That was last night. Now he rose with the sun, thinking of this good news. He breakfasted and hurried, eager to be out. Olipor had saddled his horse, but Aulus refused to ride, preferring to walk and breast the vigorous wind. It was a beautiful day, opulent with sunshine and light, possessed by a veritable gale. The road from the horse pasture was bordered on one side by a deep ravine, on the other by a mountainous forest—part of Lævinus's estate.

Looking up the cliffs and terraces, Aulus caught sight of a beautiful "look-out." At such a place a Roman loved to put a small circular temple (part temple, part summerhouse), open for the view.

"I wonder," he thought, "if I could not buy that spot from Lævinus. My fortune is sure to get better. Lævinus would sell it at a bargain."

He turned out of the road and began to clamber swiftly, strongly, up the heights. In the woods the spring flowers had secretly burst forth. Whole sheets of blue and silvery white—flowers whose stems were so delicate and hair-like that the blooms seemed hovering unsupported above the mold. It was not natural now for Aulus to sing aloud; but snatches of songs he knew kept flashing across his mind.

He reached the look-out. A glorious view westward, with the shadow of the hill on which he stood stretching far outward, and then a sunny valley where ran a tiny stream which later joined the Volturnus River. Yes, a fine look-out. He would try to buy it and add to his villa lands. He turned from the hill edge, walking farther into the forest—a level space, exquisite and fragrant with fir.

Then calamity "in aspect like the sudden night" came upon him. He plunged downward, hitting his head a terrific blow, hitting his arm yet more painfully. It took him appreciable minutes to realize where he was. Yes, in the bottom of a pit. What in the name of Jupiter did it mean? What had happened, anyway? Why did his arm hurt as it had in Numantia from a deep sword cut? What was holding him so tight? He began to struggle. Immediately his arms were gripped fast to his sides, his legs tied like a pig's for the market.

He knew now, knew at last! He was in a trap—one of those deep pits, dug by hunters to catch deer or boars. It was covered over with concealing boughs (hence he had not seen it) and contained a system of rope nets and slipnooses tied to near-by trees, which, for struggling, only grew tighter and more suffocating about the victim. He tried to move his arms. They were tied so tightly to his body that the veins stood out! And every effort only brought the nooses tighter. He began to fear that his right arm was broken, for try as he might he had no control over the fingers of his right hand.

He shouted lustily for help. After each shout came the unbroken silence of the forest. Then he stood quiet and began warily, skillfully, to twist his left hand. After a while he freed this hand from its noose, but no further effort freed it above the arm. Such traps had been developed through generations of hunting. They were clever and strong. Aulus stood still—quite still. He began coolly to review his chances of escape. Olipor would not worry if his master did not return to the midday meal. Aulus often went all day without eating. But Olipor would worry after nightfall. He would begin to search. But would he think to search in this solitary forest? Could Aulus's voice be heard from the road? Well, he would save his voice until nightfall and then begin to shout with all his might. The hunters—yes, of course the hunters would eventually visit their trap. It was a fresh trap, the earth newly turned. But how long would he have to wait for that—a day, three days, seven days? There was no telling.

Well, there was about an even chance of his dying or living. If dying, what a miserable, ignominious death! After fighting battles for three years in Numantia he had come home to die like a pig in a trap. A great wave of bitterness came over him. Reason—a god of the universe! Where was the reason of this? He was not afraid. He was very angry. Maybe after all the old gods, whom they laughed at in Rome, were real. Small, evil gods who tripped man up like this and laughed at him. Evil, evil, surely it was present in the unseen air about—present and ever ready.

For hours he stood there, his arm throbbing with pain—throbbing ever more heavily. A single sunbeam which slanted into the pit found its way to his head —then passed onward. Gradually his anger died, his mood changed. Evil! Misfortune! Ah, that old saying which Panætius had so often repeated:

"To the truly wise man no misfortune can come."

Was it possible for him (Aulus) to be wise enough to transform this silly cruelty of Fate into nothingness? Could he, here in the pit, decide that he had no misfortune? He began to try. Yes, in his cold Roman way he began to try. He actually grew interested in trying. All these months he had made artificial tests for himself, to measure his mental endurance. Here was a test made by Fate, or Nature herself. Well, he

would meet it. Suppose he should be rescued. If he
had met this misfortune bravely it would be a source
of strength and pride. He would feel self-respect.
Suppose he died. Was that to be dreaded when the
two he loved were dead and himself banished from
Rome?

Every little while he sought again to free his left
hand, his foot. He did not give up. But he was no
longer angry or afraid. He was calm and clear of
mind—serene. His long mental battle was won.

Meanwhile, for Chloé, working steadily at her
loom, the day had been one of strange impatience.
The spring wind seemed a spirit which blew through
her spirit to send it abroad. This morning had arisen
as if Youth were reborn into the very atmosphere—a
rollicking, roystering youthfulness that seized the trees
with fierce shakings. What a voice he had—this
Spirit—roaring in the forest, shrieking as he turned
a corner of the gulch below her cliff! He was Æolus,
her own Lesbian ancestor. For the people of Lesbos
traced their ancestry to this god of the winds. From
him were they born. Now she could almost see him—
this relative of her spirit, treading the top of a whole
vast forest in the vale—or again flinging himself invisible against a bare cliff, sending up dust and dry
leaves like spray against a rock. The eagle (her eagle
she knew so well) braved Æolus in mid-air and was
blown about even as the leaves were blown—now
straight upward, now in a swift slant almost to the
ground—wings spread and still. Joy it was to the

eagle to be so buffeted. Joy would it have been to
Chloé to be buffeted also. But, alas, it was not herself but her threads that Æolus caught and blew
this way and that.

"Chloé!" called Melissa from the hut. "You know
well that your fabric will be ruined if you stay out
of doors with your loom."

"Mischief take my fabric!" Chloé answered impatiently. "I do not want to come in."

"You are very foolish," said Melissa.

Chloé knew of course that she must go into the
hut. She took a long look at the world-spread valley,
with its racing cloud shadows, its far Elysiums of
sunny meadow. Then she began strongly to drag her
loom into the hut. Melissa came to help her. Together they brought it in. Then Melissa closed and
bolted the door. Chloé resumed her work by the light
of the chimney hole.

But even so, Æolus invaded the hut. He shook the
door and knocked upon it, calling to Chloé, "Come
out. Come out."

Chloé began to work as fast as ever she could. She
must finish her stint of the day and get out into her
beloved forest. Never had she been so urged. She
always believed afterward that Æolus really had
called her forth; that she herself had somehow sensed
a need which her mortal mind did not know. People
of Chloé's temperament are apt to believe such things
where others would see nothing but natural cause.
Yet who shall deny them their belief? She omitted

her midday meal for haste. Early in the afternoon she set down her shuttle with sudden decision.

"I am going out," she said to Melissa. "I cannot stay in the hut."

She put on the short tunic she always wore for running in the wood—the one which Melissa had woven of wool from their own sheep. So she hurried forth.

CHAPTER 20

To the Truly Wise Man No Misfortune
Can Come

To the truly wise man no misfortune can come.
Stoic saying

Aulus had grown weary in the pit trap. He was almost overcome with sleep. Truly in the whole calendar of Rome there was not a day so long as this. Not a day so unlucky. He tried to recall whether any ill omen had crossed his path, any bird flying, any stubbing of his toe upon the threshold. There was absolutely none. How foolish omens were anyway.

Suddenly the silence of the forest was broken by a song—clear song in Sapphic meter, as beautiful as anything Aulus had ever heard. Great Jupiter, were the spirits of the dead coming for him already! He shook himself free of sleep. Then he began to call lustily with all the strength of his lungs:

"Help! I am in the pit. Here on top of the hill. Help!"

Instantly the song ceased. He called again in the silence. Then footsteps running, running. Thankfulness such as Aulus had never known swept over him like an actual cloud of brightness. The sudden let-go of Fate, of misery—Death itself! He was saved.

Someone was tearing away the branches at the top of the pit. Then a face bent over—the flushed, wondering face of a girl.

"Go fetch help from the Villa Cornelia," he commanded.

"Oh——" It was a long, horrified shudder. "*You* instead of the stag! You to be caught!"

That instant she leaped into the pit beside him. Aulus was suddenly so angry that he felt like striking her.

"Why in the name of the gods did you do that?" he demanded. "Now we are both caught."

"Oh, no," she answered, "I was sent to save you."

"But your feet are in the net!" he cried, almost tearful with disappointment.

Sure enough. She bent over. Her strong, deft fingers, so accustomed to tangled threads, soon undid the noose and freed her feet. Indeed it was a slight bit of the net that had caught her. Then to Aulus's amazement she grasped the sapling which her leap had dragged in with her, swung herself to it, and clambered out like a squirrel.

"Wait," she called. "They usually leave a knife for the ropes."

He could hear her digging among the dry leaves.

"Yes, yes, here it is!" Her voice had a catch of joy.

Then she leaped down again, swift and squirrel-like as before, and began to cut the ropes. Great

Jupiter, the relief of it! And the girl worked as though she were fairly possessed with haste—breathless, impatient. As she freed his right arm the pain shot up into his shoulder and neck.

"Oh," she cried out again with pity. "It is broken! It is broken!"

"My sword arm!" thought Aulus bitterly. To Roman as to Greek that was the first use of man's right arm and hand. The sculptor's hand, the writer's, the artificer's, the physician's is never mentioned.

Now the girl was freeing his legs. The dead numbness of them gave way to burning and tingling. Swiftly, deftly, with the sharp hunting knife, she cut the ropes. He began to stretch his legs to get life back into them.

"Now!" she breathed at last, as if the relief were her own. Then with her same amazing quickness she climbed up the slanted sapling. Aulus with his left hand tested the slender branching trunk—decided it was strong enough—and, one-armed as he was, climbed slowly out.

Oh, the wonder, the joy to be in the sunshine again, standing erect! It was like coming out of the grave. Aulus drew a long, long breath of the pure air and of thankfulness at the same time. He was aware that the slave girl was standing shy and silent, as if half afraid of him now he was himself again.

"I have not even thanked you," Aulus said kindly. "But you have saved my life. I shall certainly give you an award."

He saw a flush pass over her face, as if he had

said the wrong thing. But she could not be other than a slave girl—running about alone in the wood in that short tunic of hers. She was a pretty creature —like some wild fawn or doe.

"How did you happen to come so far into the wood?" he asked.

She hesitated, timid at saying what she thought to be true.

"I was told to come."

"Told! But who on earth could know?"

"Oh, they knew quite well. They kept telling me all morning. If only I had obeyed sooner!"

"But who?"

"It might have been Æolus," she explained. "Or a nymph. You cannot always tell just who it is."

Of course, this was sheer nonsense to Aulus. He wondered if the girl was right in her head.

"Well, I must go home," he said, with a glance at his helpless arm.

"Please, Master Cornelius," said Chloé, humbly and quite like a slave. "Melissa could mend your arm."

"Who is Melissa?" he demanded.

"My friend, my mother's friend. She mended Psappha's leg—— Oh," she hastened to add, seeing utter puzzlement in his face, "not our great beautiful Psappha of Lesbos who died so long ago. Psappha is our goat. After Melissa mended her she could run and leap as well as her daughter Cleis."

Aulus was troubled about his arm. It must be set rightly. There was a man in Aufidena who pretended to cure, but Aulus had heard of his terrible bungling.

"Where is your Melissa?" he asked.

"At home in our hut."

"Will you bring her to me?"

She nodded—such a glad assent. She turned, then looked back at him.

"You won't go away?" She seemed afraid of losing him.

"Of course not."

Then she leaped forward and was soon lost in the forest.

In some twenty minutes she was back again, bringing with her a thin, thoughtful-faced woman whom somehow Aulus trusted.

"Are you the woman who cared for Olipor's hand when it was crushed in the olive press?" he inquired. He had remembered suddenly that Olipor had told him of a woman living on Lævinus's estate, better than anyone in the country round.

"Yes, master." But already Melissa was touching his arm, skillful and interested. She clucked with her tongue.

"I hoped Chloé was wrong. It *is* broken. If you can, master, it would be well to come to my home, where I have water and splints and bandages."

"Is it far?"

"No, master."

"Then show me the way."

Melissa walked with him as if to protect him from stumbling. But the slave girl darted on ahead, searching for the best footway. They came to a stream. She made them ascend its bank a little way to a ford. Melissa waded in ahead of him. He supposed the girl would follow. But he saw her seize a hanging vine and, with a single leap, go flying across to the opposite bank. In spite of the throbbing pain in his arm, Aulus was charmed at such skill.

"You are a strange creature," he commented. "I'll begin to think you are a nymph as you said a while ago."

"But I did not say that," she answered, troubled. "There is a nymph in this wood, but it is not I."

Then they were at the hut. Such a strange, lonely place at the foot of a crag. They gave him a seat near the door. Then how they hastened at their work for him, Melissa directing, Chloé helping! Chloé brought water in a basin. Melissa washed Aulus's arm. Melissa cut the flat smooth rods from her loom for splints, while Chloé brought soft linen. Then, sitting, knee braced against his knee, Melissa with a fiery wrench pulled the bones straight.

"Hold it," she commanded Chloé. "Hold his arm steady."

"The girl can never do it," thought Aulus.

But the minute her strong, supple hands took hold he knew she could. It was a serious business for Aulus. His whole future as a swordsman and a soldier depended upon Melissa's skill. He was thankful to see she was deft and quick. The process was painful. However, that was all in a day's work for a Roman soldier. He was quite sure he did not flinch—but every time a torment seized him he saw the flicker of it in the girl's eyes, a veritable echo. It was as if she made the pain her own, meeting his soul midway. Aulus did not think of this at the time. He remembered it afterward.

At last it was done. Melissa like a mother washed the sweat from Aulus's face with the cool water.

"How long were you in the pit?" she asked.

"Since morning."

"Then you are hungry."

What a curious experience it was for Aulus, sitting there by that very poor hut on the lonely mountainside, and being waited upon by two women he had never seen before. Never had goat's milk tasted so rich and sweet, never was cheese so sharp of tang, or honey so freshly fragrant. Aulus was famished and ate like a boy. And the women both took such pleasure in serving him. When he spoke of reward, Melissa replied: "Please do not reward us. We have no need of anything."

Aulus realized that both Melissa and the girl had been speaking an ancient form of Greek—perhaps Æolic—and that he had been responding in the speech of Athens.

In the midst of his meal the goats and ewes came bleating home. Chloé called to them by name and led them into their fold. Was it already evening— folding time? How the hours had flown! And when he rose to go, Chloé knew a path through the wood that led directly to the Caracinia garden and thence to his own horse pasture. She led him thither, going ahead of him as before. They reached the break in the wall.

"You have added kindness to kindness," said Aulus. "And you will take nothing in return."

"It is reward enough just to know that I saved you," she said.

Then with a lifting of the hand for good-bye she was gone into the wood.

What a strange answer for a slave girl to make! And why was it so familiar to him, the lustrous look of her dark eyes? Where had he seen it before? He of course did not associate it with Kæso in Rome. He crossed the pasture toward the villa. The peace which he had won in the pit's imprisonment was still with him. Could it be that he had been gone from the house only a day? It seemed a year, a long, strange time-space of change.

"To the truly wise man no misfortune can come."

He said this almost happily as he crossed the threshold of his lonely home.

CHAPTER 21

Upon the Topmost Bough

The sweet apple blushes upon the topmost bough.
                                                  Sappho

Something had happened to Aulus's thinking. It was more vital, directed. The eternal pull of lonely grief which in all his hours he had had to meet and ignore had somehow lost power, and in its stead was a feeling of friendliness in the world. He determined to send to Cornelia the next time Bion went to Rome, asking for some books upon oratory and the law. Even if he were banished from Rome he could make himself an orator and a lawyer. He could, since matters had become safer, go into Aufidena or Sulmona and try cases at the law, and thus win skill, so that if he was ever allowed to return to the great city he would be equipped for a career. No Roman ever charged for legal work. But to be a lawyer was the height of Roman ambition. It was perhaps the finest trait of Roman character—this pride in producing justice.

Aulus wondered at the change in himself. Could the pit experience mean so much to him? He decided that it was partly because now he must sit so quiet with his broken arm. Meanwhile he picked up his Euripides, reading those heart-stirring plays, remembering the time when he had seen certain of them in the glorious, sun-filled theater at Athens.

So passed a number of days. Then the arm bones began to knit, and with that came annoying pain. At night he lay awake long hours or fell into a fitful sleep in which he constantly dreamed he was again in the pit. He had felt some satisfaction in that dread experience. The worst had happened to him, and he had met it with equanimity. His Stoic thinking had availed. He had a certain new trust in himself. So he felt when broad awake and rational. But now in this fevered sleep he was always in the horror of the pit. Abject terror would seize him, abject fear of death. Then suddenly would come the face of the slave girl gleaming over the edge of the pit. Suddenly again she would be in the pit beside him, cutting one band after another, her pretty dark head bent so near him at the task. Rope after rope she cut and freed him so. Then the dream would become more confused; the girl was freeing him from prisonhoods of thought, strange conditions which he could not explain. All these she cut with the knife and set him free. Then suddenly she flew across his consciousness, lovely, birdlike, and swift, as she had leaped across the stream.

This awoke him. Aulus would curse his foolishness and try to go to sleep again.

One morning after a particularly bad night Aulus determined to go and see the woman-leech again. Olipor had assured him that she was the best healer in the region. The slaves at Villa Cornelia often went to her for help, and she was usually successful. Perhaps the arm was not acting right. He must make sure. He took his way across the horse pasture, up the hill, and to the break in Lævinus's garden wall. Here was the direct path through the wood.

As he neared the hut, he became aware that the girl was singing. The sound pierced easily through the forest silences, the voice so pure that one almost mistook its purity for emotion. Now, nearer, he could hear the words—Attic Greek with an Æolic mistake now and then:

> "*Under the arched cliffs, O were I lying,*
> *That then to a bird might a god change me.*
> *I would fly afar, winged among the wingèd,*
> *Over the Adrian Sea.*
> *I would poise aloft, dreaming upon my wings,*
> *Over the waters of Eridanus,*
> *Where, down upon the purple surge of the sea,*
> *Rain the tears of the Sun-god's daughters,*
> *Grieving for Phaëton their Brother,*
> *Star flashes and amber.*"

By Pollux, the girl was singing a chorus from Hippolytus. He had been reading the play only yesterday. But how in heaven's name could an ignorant girl like that know Hippolytus? The path emerged suddenly. Aulus broke through the bushes right beside the goatfold and in full view of the hut. The loom stood in front of the door, set with brilliant colors, and before it the girl darted back and forth, throwing the shuttle, so busily singing she did not know his presence until he spoke.

Then she whirled about—such an expression in her face that he could not tell whether she would run toward him or away. She did neither, but it took her an appreciable minute to remember her manners.

"You are welcome, Master Cornelius," she said.

"Is your Melissa here?" Aulus asked. "I have come to let her look at my arm."

"Oh, is it worse?"

"No, but it could be more comfortable."

"I'll fetch her," said Chloé and hurried off down to the stream, where Melissa was pressing the cheese.

Left alone, Aulus looked curiously about him. The place was exquisitely neat. The two looms side by side under the rustic porch, Melissa's set with white wool, Chloé's with purple and carmine. The place had changed with the advance of spring. A wild-apple tree had bloomed perhaps that morning. It looked new-made enough for that, thrusting its plucky trunk from the base of the cliff and lifting white branches abroad—casting a whitish shade. And glory to the gods! What a view from the cliff! There should be a villa here instead of a slave hut.

Chloé came back.

"Melissa will hasten," she reported. "She says will you kindly stay for the *cena*. But you must not, if our food is too poor. You could get far better; that I know."

"The last meal I had here was the best I ever tasted," he answered.

"Ah, you were hungry!" She laughed at the memory of his eager eating, and Aulus laughed with her. It was more comradely than he intended.

Chloé began to set upon a flat stone their little collection of bowls and their one single spoon.

The Romans (even those who loved luxury for themselves) took great delight in rusticity in others. The scene reminded Aulus of Theocritus. "And by Juno," he thought, "isn't she Greek? Strange how you can tell them in every movement they make."

"By the way," he spoke suddenly, "how do you happen to sing Hippolytus?"

She blushed rosy all over her face. Aulus could not imagine why the question should so embarrass her. He could not guess that he himself was her Hippolytus.

"Because—you see—Bion saw the play in Athens and—and he told it to Melissa and I listened. I know all the lines Bion knows, but they are so few."

"Do you know any other plays?"

"Yes, but, oh, so little of each one. Melissa told me the lines where Alkestis comes back from Death, and where Ion sweeps the threshold of the temple. I say them over and over as I work. I wish—I wish I knew more."

Melissa now came hastening as she had promised. She brought a bowl of water and fresh linen. Sitting before him knee to knee, she took off the outer bandage.

"Does it look straight?" he inquired anxiously. "Will it be useful again?"

"It is knitting perfectly. The best I ever saw. In a few months you will not know it happened."

Aulus sighed relief.

"I'll never go into battle without thinking of you, Melissa," he said devoutly. To Aulus it was perfectly natural to look forward to battle and carnage.

She washed the arm, adjusted the splints, and bound it up with fresh linen. The refreshment was great. Then came the meal. They waited upon him, standing servantwise, but he could not but feel their companionship. After his lonely meals at the villa, with the eternal empty chair of his mother—this experience kept up a slow, unconscious reheartening of him.

"And what more do you know besides Euripides?" he asked, looking up amusedly at Chloé.

"I know what Melissa has taught me," she answered. "And Melissa knows—oh—everything!"

"Tut, tut, child!" admonished Melissa. "The master will think I do nothing but waste time."

"Not when your loom stands so full," said Aulus kindly.

"Her father was exegete of the temple in Eresus," went on Chloé proudly. "So he had to know all the stories of the gods and all the traditions of Lesbos. And he knew all the poetry as well. He gave it to Melissa, and so it came down to me."

"Lesbos!" spoke Aulus with quick shining in his face. "I went there from Athens. Gods, what an island! What a proud empire all to itself! Like a tiny jewel in the sea."

It was so unexpected, that name, that praise, that Melissa's eyes filled with tears. She hid her face. As for Chloé, her face blossomed into tenderness. Aulus felt as though he had opened an unexpected door. These slaves—Lesbians! What a shame! And it explained them, too.

"I did not mean to hurt you," he said.

"Oh, no, no, you have not," faltered Melissa. But she could not speak further. She hurried away with the dishes.

"You must not mind that," spoke Chloé softly. "It is because she longs for Lesbos always—and I do, too."

Aulus rose from the table—the slab of stone, rather. He knew it was time to go. But curiously he did not want to go. At home was a lonely room, a lonely portico, some scrolls he had read twenty times. Somehow, at this moment, he hated them all. They seemed dead—the scrolls, too.

"Do you," he inquired slowly, "know the song of the sweet apple—Sappho's?"

Instantly she began to sing it—softly, almost whisperingly, as if not wanting Melissa to hear. As indeed she did not. Melissa knew the danger of her singing so to a young Roman.

> *"As the sweet apple blushes on the topmost bough*
> *The very end of the bough,*
> *Which the pluckers forgot somehow,*
> *Nay, forgot not*
> *But could not reach."*

The song is lost now. But Chloé knew the precious whole of it—the fair ideals of the soul beyond reach of the soul, named one after another in lyric mixed with fire. And love, the highest ideal of all, like the supreme moon in the sky.

> *"The stars about the fair moon*
> *Each in its turn*
> *Hides and is quenched*
> *In the deep empyrean.*
> *While she, full clear and round,*
> *Lights all the earth with silver."*

The words came through the undervoiced singing as distinct as speech; but with a depth of meaning which never speech possessed. It was *living*—that song. Living like the new-blossomed tree, the new-blossomed girl beneath the tree. Great Juno! Had Aulus thought he was reading poetry off a scroll when this source of song lay so near! Even Panætius could do nothing like this.

Melissa came back.

"I must be going," Aulus said to her hurriedly. "I stay longer than I mean. After all I'm sole-alone at home. Perhaps" (he seemed a little confused, as well he might be) "you will both sing me some traditions of Lesbos. Such things should not be lost."

He hurried away to the path and clambered out of sight.

"Chloé," said Melissa, provoked almost to tears. "Now why did you sing to him like that?"

"He asked me."

"But you need not have sung that song."

"He asked me to sing that song."

"Well, then, you needn't have sung it in the way you did. You have never sung so before."

"Oh, Melissa, *did* I sing it well? It seemed as though I were singing it well. I forgot everything else."

"You sang it all too well," said Melissa. And in sudden tenderness for what was beyond her help and Chloé's, she kissed her.

CHAPTER 22

The Play, Hippolytus

The song followed Aulus home every step of the way. He found himself walking to its rhythm. It was as if he had never heard it before—such newness of meaning, newness of life. Yes, that was the word—newness of life. Aulus had been taught that love was at best a foolish and dangerous passion. But in this song, love was different from that. High and eternal. It was like—why, it was like Plato's Beauty.

"I wonder if the girl knows Plato." He smiled to himself. Euripides, Sappho, Plato. Pretty liberal education for a slave girl. He sought his favorite portico, brought out his precious Symposium and began to read the conversation of Diotima. It scintillated with new meaning all through as if that Sapphic song had vitalized it. He read happily until supper time. The next day it was raining. Perhaps that was why Aulus was suddenly depressed and felt the vacancy of his day. If he could only have galloped forth on his favorite mare all would have been well. But that was of course impossible in the present state of his arm. He paced the atrium impatiently. Suddenly he thought, "I'll go up to the mountain hut. That's the thing!" He had actually started for his cloak when he stopped himself, angry now in earnest. Was he growing to be dependent upon two slave women for company? It was all very well for him to go there for treatment of his arm; but to go for companionship was rank foolishness. Verania had brought her sons up with sedulous care. She particularly disliked association with slaves. Even in their early childhood she had kept her two boys with high-born boys for playmates. "Thus it becomes habit," Aulus had often heard her say. When Gnæus had begun going with slave women it had almost broken her heart. And indeed Gnæus had never been the same afterward. Never really fine or honest. And now! Of course, these two mountain women were innocent creatures—not like the slaves of Rome; but they were slaves nevertheless.

Aulus tossed his coat back upon its peg, took up his Plato and began to read. It was duller than he ever supposed Plato could be. He slid over to his Euripides; Hippolytus was more to the point. He wondered how much of it Chloé really knew. It would be interesting to test her with the lines. This line, for instance, and this, where Hippolytus dies. The next time he went he would—

"By Juno, there will be no next time!"

Aulus jumped from his seat and banged the scroll upon the floor. Was this an evil possession? This cursed lonely villa was playing tricks on him. He had almost the notion to go back to Rome at any risk.

That afternoon Bion came in. An unexpected trip to Rome, and Bion would carry messages. Aulus wrote out, as well as he could with his left hand, the lawbooks he desired from Cornelia. Bion inquired respectfully about Aulus's arm.

"It is doing well. The slave woman over at your villa tended it. And she is skillful."

"Yes, you can trust her," responded Bion. "I've known her to save patients that the Aufidena doctor had given up."

"By the way, Bion," said Aulus suddenly, "who is she? Lesbian, so she says. But where was she bought?"

"She wasn't bought, master," said Bion. He seemed now curiously unwilling to talk of her.

"What then?"

"She was captured."

"Who captured her?"

"Well, master—Lævinus captured her long ago in a raid against pirates in Lesbos."

"Lævinus!" Aulus's interest was fired at once. "Then it was she who was Lævinus's lady-love."

"Oh, no, no, master," Bion said hurriedly. "Chloé was his—lady-love. But here in the villa we say, 'his wife.'"

"Chloé? Gods in Olympus, Chloé is too young." Aulus felt himself grow hot all over at this thought of Chloé's wrong.

"No, please, master. Not this Chloé—but Chloé the Lesbian. Melissa was her friend."

"Then who in the name of thunder is this Chloé?"

Yet more unwilling was Bion. But he said it at last:

"She is Lævinus's daughter."

It came like the name of thunder which Aulus had invoked.

"Lævinus's daughter!" he repeated. "Lævinus's daughter!" He began to pace the floor. "Then she isn't a slave." He little knew how much joy came into his face, saying this.

"Well, we don't know, master. Lævinus married her mother by the foreign rite. That we know. He set her up as *matrona* of the villa. Then he suddenly repudiated her, and married Helvia. So they tell me. I was away for many years at another estate."

"But the daughter—the daughter. How dare he leave her in such a situation? She is his own flesh and blood."

"Yes, master; but perhaps he does not even know of her birth. That was after he left the villa."

"Of course he knows. He is marvelous careful not to come down here, isn't he?"

Bion said nothing. He was wishing with all his heart that the two women had not come to the young patrician's notice. There was no telling—— But Aulus was prodding him again.

"Do they call her a slave—these at the villa?"

"Melissa? Well, that is a question—her status——"

"No, no, no! The girl. It's the girl I'm asking about."

"I am afraid they do. At least they did until I came. Davus had beaten her until she was nearly dead."

"Beaten her!—not this beautiful delicate child, Chloé!"

Aulus was so moved that he did not stop to question why or how much. It was a horror, a shrinking as though he himself had been struck. And he was so angry that his face frightened the gentle Bion.

"In god's name why did he beat her?"

"Because she could not do the tasks he assigned her. They were twice as much as a child could do."

Aulus was walking up and down the room. He did not dismiss Bion, so Bion still stood, watching him with amazement.

The new knowledge beat around in Aulus's mind like an imprisoned bird. Now this aspect of it, now that, flashing up.

"Did she live with the slaves?" he demanded. How terrible if this Roman girl had been subjected to the degrading life of slave quarters!

"No, master. Always, up in that little hut, Melissa holds herself above the slaves, and has so held Chloé, keeping her separate."

Aulus breathed a perfectly heard sigh of relief.

"Of course," ventured Bion, "you must have noticed her resemblance to Lævinus." Bion felt this would serve Chloé.

Aulus was unaccountably indignant.

"Indeed not. She does not look the least like him. Not the least." (That flower of a girl like old Lævinus—he guessed not!) Aulus suddenly realized that he was showing undue excitement.

"I'll tell you, Bion. I don't want it known around.

The slaves would talk. But this young Chloé saved
my life. It was she found me in a stag trap. She
fished me out. It was then I had broken my arm. I
am naturally grateful to her."

"Yes, master," said Bion.

Then Aulus dismissed him.

In spite of the rain, Aulus went out to walk the
muddy roads. He was happy. It no longer seemed
necessary to shame himself for enjoying the society
of this girl and this kindly woman. The girl might
have been his neighbor on the Palatine. She might,
if she had had her rights, have lived always just a
few doors away from him in Rome. Of course in that
case he would have seen her hardly at all. Perhaps
he might have sat at table with her among the two
families, seen her playing knucklebones with his sisters, passed her on the street, she holding fast her
mother's hand. There would have been no companionship. Girls were stupid. They had no life outside
the house. Lavinia, for instance—what a pale, word-
less little creature! Chloé's half-sister, by Juno!
Aulus's own sisters could read, but what good did it
do them? They never read the scrolls, only did household accounts. They weren't alive like Chloé. They
would no more sing a Sapphic song than they would
dance a fantastic on the house top. As for Chloé's
lonely romantic situation, the tragedy of it was like
a piece of poetry.

Grateful to her? Of course he was grateful and
had every right to be. And he wished, the very Roman wish, to give for value received. One thing he

could do: he could *buy* Chloé and Melissa from Lævinus and set them free. Some day he would have money enough. If not, he could sell two of the villa slaves and so get the price. Freedom would protect Chloé from any such cursed experience as she had had. And Aulus would so protect her. He would indeed.

So he planned and thought and planned again.

Next morning Aulus did not make up his mind to go to the hut: it was quite made up when he awoke; and he went about it with perfect naturalness. Put on a fresh tunic (one did not wear a toga in the country), took his scroll of Hippolytus in his hand and went. He was so early that they were still setting the warps of the looms. Melissa received him with a shadow of anxiety, Chloé as though the morning had that moment dawned.

"Don't stop your work," he said kindly. "It was lonely at the villa. And I wearied sitting still. So I thought I would watch you."

He sat down on a flat rock, opened his scroll and pretended to read.

How deftly Chloé worked! That Melissa also worked deftly did not concern him. Just as she handled those threads of the warp, so had her fingers handled the twisted ropes in the pit. Now she was fastening the long bright threads of linen to the broad linen-weaving loom, selecting the purple threads with infinite care, counting these as she tied them to the pegs and weighted them at the bottom with stones. To Aulus it seemed only caprice, the selection of colors. Every little while Chloé stole a look at him as if to make sure he was really there.

"Why do you put in purple threads?" he asked.

"Because they are the dragon. His scales are to be purple and yellow. The yellow threads, though, are on the shuttle."

"Are you making a picture of it?"

"Yes, it is for a couch covering, or, if I make it well enough, to hang upon a wall. It is Apollo slaying the dragon. I love this one."

Suddenly occurred to Aulus the skill of what she was doing: carrying a picture or pattern in her mind and laying its foundations among these blind, meaningless threads.

The whole place and the two women looked strange to Aulus this morning. He was having to re-think, re-see everything. This was no longer a miserable slave hut, it was a place of secret meanings which no one but himself knew. He was re-seeing Chloé—not slave girl now, but Roman girl. To a high-bred Roman it made the difference of night and day. Upon a slave there was degradation which amounted to a curse. This had lifted from Chloé. But try as he might, he could not see her as Roman. She was too tall, slender, too swift of movement. She seemed all Greek. The way her hair rippled back from her temples—it was like that statue in Lævinus's garden (Aulus had seen it that morning). Yes, by Jove, she was like that old Greek statue, and her long brown slave dress had the grace of Athena's chiton. There was a great hole on one shoulder, poor little girl!

She had finished the warp. And stood up straight with a sigh.

"Can't you rest now a moment?" he asked.

She glanced at Melissa as if for permission.

"I have brought my Hippolytus. You said you wanted to know more of it."

She came toward him with eyes like a child before whom you hold a bright treasure.

"Will you," she said, marveling—"will you give me more of the lines?"

"Sit down," he said. Somehow he did not want her to stand before him slavewise. He spread out the scroll.

"Oh, here is a chorus especially for you," he exclaimed. And read to her:

>"'A rock there is wherefrom as they tell
>   The springs of the heart of Ocean dwell.
>   Even there did I light on a maiden (my friend),
>   As she drenched the mantles purple gleaming
>   In the river, the glittering spray,
>   And spread the dye of the Tyrian shell
>   On the rocks where sunbeams fell.'"

The deep silence of the place was broken only by Aulus's voice reading and the continual pouring sound of the waterfall.

"By Zeus," he said, as he had finished. "When I sit here in this forest, it doesn't seem as though Rome exists."

"Would you rather be in Rome?" she asked.

He shook his head. The fever and noise of the Forum, the cruel rivalry, the selfishness, the murder of Tiberius—all came over his consciousness with a sort of horror. Chloé read it quick in his face.

"He hates Rome, where they seek to kill him," she decided. "He will stay here always, where I can see him and hear his voice. He will stay here, here!"

Her heart swelled with joy. She took for a reality what was in Aulus a passing mood. It was to mean much in the after event.

"Now what part of the play shall I read you?" asked Aulus.

"Read," she said eagerly, "where the father curses Hippolytus, and where, dying, he forgives his father."

The chaste tragedy, so poisoned in modern versions, was there in its early purity, its heart-rending drama. It was concerned only with the swift-riding, forest-loving Hippolytus, whose worship of the forest-goddess Artemis, provokes the anger of Aphrodite. Aphrodite wrecks the boy through his stepmother Phædra. Theseus, the father, believing the lies against his son, invokes the curse of Poseidon upon him. Then Hippolytus calls for his chariot and horses and sorrowfully but swiftly rides away.

The beauty of the play lies in Hippolytus's terrific ride to the sea beach.

> "Then a surge unearthly
> Rose from the sea like a column
> And sprayed on the beach Scironion."

Out of this high white wave came a Shape of
Fear, as if all the cruelty and awe of wide Ocean
were focused into it. The horses went stark mad.
They dashed Hippolytus from the chariot, dragged
him tangled in the reins over bush and stone. Broken
and dying, he is borne back to his father's house.
Theseus meanwhile has learned of the innocence of
his son and yearns in grief toward him. Hippolytus,
gentle (lifted as it were above earth), forgives his
father. The scene is unique in Greek writing. In the
avenging temper of the ancient world it seems like a
foretaste of Christ.

As Aulus read this he could see Chloé's lips form-
ing the words with him, so intent that sometimes
she murmured the words aloud.

"Do you want to learn it?" Aulus asked.

"If you read again slowly, I will know some of it,"
she said.

He read the scenes once more. Melissa dropped
her work and listened, too. It was not in her to
resist this Greek beauty.

Then, before Aulus realized it, they were all three
acting the play together. Melissa was the Chorus,
she was also the messenger who tells of the dramatic
ride. She did this in a fashion that made Aulus know
wherefrom Chloé had got teaching. Aulus himself
was Hippolytus because Chloé insisted:

"You *are* Hippolytus, because you ride the beautiful horses."

Chloé was Theseus, the repentant father.

Aulus had to read his part from the scroll. But Chloé and Melissa gave theirs free. They left out a line here and there, others they extemporized. But the important lines were perfect. The essential poetry was there. It was Aulus's first experience of the power of primitive memory.

Surely Aulus had never read as he was reading now, with feeling, rhythm, a visioning of the part. He could not do otherwise, because Chloé responded with such quick reality. The heartbreak of Theseus, his repentance and father love, leaped in her voice. The horror of Hippolytus's broken body was reflected back into the shrinking look of her face. When Aulus responded he forgot entirely to be self-conscious.

Then came a new character. Suddenly Chloé was the goddess Artemis. That was most wonderful of all. Aulus, as the dying Hippolytus, announced her:

> "'Ah, perfume-breath celestial!
> 'Mid my pains
> I feel thee, and mine anguish is assuaged.
> Lo, in this place the Goddess Artemis!'"

Chloé as Artemis answered:

> "'Yea, hapless one, thy friend among the gods.'"

There was something absolutely cloud-like in her advance, weightless in her poise; and her eyes saw afar as a goddess sees.

There followed a most exquisite dialogue of short sentences. Artemis, praising her worshiper, adjuring him to forgive his father, vowing vengeance on the cruel Aphrodite: Hippolytus responding with renewed worship. Then the death pangs come upon Hippolytus, and Artemis hides her face from what an Immortal may not look upon.

For a moment they were silent, all of them. Then Chloé spread wide her arms as if to free herself of illusion.

"Oh, I am so glad you are not dead!" she cried, with a face still wet with tears.

CHAPTER 23

As the Tree Blooms

At home in the villa Aulus laughed merrily over this experience. That he, a sober Roman, should have spent the morning play-acting with two women! Of course, he had made a fool of himself trying to act his part—by Jupiter, he had forgotten the foolishness of it in the vividness of that grand old play. Surely the Greeks knew how to deal with their own. Melissa had carried off the Chorus with grand rhythm. And Chloé!—Was ever anything as lovely as that first moment of her Artemis! Aulus laughed again, appreciatively—a laugh of happiness.

It did not occur to him how strange it was for him to laugh at all. He who had come up to this villa with his youth dead within him. Youth for Aulus had died in that moment when Tiberius was killed. His trust in life, his enthusiasm to meet it, died then. And with his mother's death the same day all the sweetness of childhood had gone down in darkness. In such death of the spirit he had come to the villa. So he had dwelt all winter. Now youth was reborn. He was not at all aware of it. Its very naturalness deceived him. Besides, it was not like the youth he had lost. It was more vigorous, fuller of mental delight. All his faculties came keen and alert. When the books of law arrived from Cornelia he attacked them with vigor. When an actual law case presented itself in Aufidena, he undertook it, saw through his opponent's motives, and argued the case so well that he won it. It was to Chloé that he took his triumph. Indeed there was no other in the world to care. And she cared supremely. Even when alone in the villa Aulus no longer felt alone but somehow companioned by Chloé on the hill. And quite naturally he fell into the habit of climbing along the forest path that led to the hut. Sometimes he brought the white bread of the villa—a treat for them—and shared the meal, sitting with them as he had not done at first. Once he brought delicate wine. But Chloé would not touch it. This pleased him. No Roman girl should drink wine. His arm knitted at last. Melissa took off the splints. It was straight and normal.

"Your arm is yours," said Chloé joyously, "but its rightness and strength belong to Melissa and me."

"How is that?" he inquired, very happy because of the arm, very grateful because of the arm.

"I do not know. It is a joy that is inside us. Something that is ours because we helped to make it exist. It is mine, anyway."

"That is a Platonic thought. Rightness all by itself—existent. Do you know Plato, too?"

"I know that he was wise and good and that he was once a slave and that the price of his freedom was given back to Athens, so they bought a beautiful grove with it. And there he taught."

"I have seen the grove," he said. "I have walked under Plato's trees."

Aulus somehow took for granted all Chloé's outspoken joy in his coming. It was a childlike joy. He had never seen her without it, and he took it for a habit of her mind, not particularly associating himself with it. But the warmth of that love was a healing to which he came as men come to healing waters. Day after day he came and went home warmed and healed of the hurts of Rome.

Once he asked Chloé suddenly:

"Why do you say I am Hippolytus? You never saw me ride."

"Oh, yes—yes, I have," she answered.

"But when?"

"Long ago. You rode two horses at once, in the pasture."

"You saw that! How?"

Then she had to confess her secret watching from the broken wall. It touched him strangely, the lonely child watching day after day the happiness she might not share. He felt again indignant against Lævinus who had left her so.

"Did you see my mother, too?" he inquired.

"Yes, I always pretended she was my friend and talked with her. You see she is so beautiful and young that I imagine my mother was like her."

"But she is dead. Did not you know that?"

"Oh, no, no—not my lady Verania?" she cried.

She was as stricken as though Verania had been close to her in real friendship. Her face was full of grief.

He told her the story. How he had come home from the death of Tiberius and how Verania had died in his arms. She in her turn told of the times she had seen Verania watch for him hours before he came, the times she looked down the road at his departing and gestured a blessing out of the air.

"Did she do that?" he asked tenderly.

"Yes, every time."

It was a new memory of his mother—a new touch with her—her who he thought had gone beyond all touch. He and Chloé shared this.

So the intimacy grew. Melissa was still disturbed by it. Yet she could not but like the honesty of Aulus and his frank behavior. As for Chloé, she lived in a bright dream into which she entered deeper and deeper, until Aulus was as some golden atmosphere closing her in from the world.

Then one day came a farmer from Sulmona. He was being cheated of his farm, the mortgage holder trying unjustly to foreclose.

"I heard of the law case in Aufidena," he said to Aulus, "and how you won it. I thought maybe you would in your great kindness get justice for me."

The case presented some peculiar difficulties, which Aulus attacked with ardor. He took long walks, thrashing them out. He studied his books. He wrote his conclusions. He altered his conclusions. Then came the suit. He traveled to Sulmona and won it. All this took more than a fortnight. Roman-like, perhaps manlike, Aulus did not think to explain his absence from the hut. He did not think of his presence there as important. He was not a conceited man, and had too ready an admiration for others to be self-centered. That was one reason why the centering upon himself in thought through the winter had been so sore a trial. Even Chloé's outshining love for him had not penetrated this modesty—or was it pride, which never for a moment had let him think of love between himself and the humble Chloé? Meanwhile his absence had wrought desolation.

After the third day Chloé began watching the path, looking up wistfully from her work. The work itself became unbearable in loneliness and monotony. Melissa tried to comfort her, saying the worst thing in the world:

"I warned you, Chloé. If only you would not fix your mind upon that young man."

Chloé worked on.

"And after all he is a Roman and will act as Romans always do."

"No, no, don't call him a Roman. It is just as if he were not Roman at all. He is banished and will never go back to Rome. He hates it as I do."

"He is thoroughly Roman," insisted Melissa. "We have done favors for him. He will take them as a matter of course, with no gratitude. Oh, Chloé, nothing but ill can come from this friendship. You know well—the best he could do—if he even cared to do that much—would be to buy you as slave, and as slave take you to Rome, where, when he tires of you, he will cast you to destruction."

"How dare you say such cruel things of him! He is good—good!" said Chloé, beginning to weep.

"Yes, he is good, but he is not good for you. He considers you a miserable slave girl, who chances to please him for a moment."

Melissa let this sink in. Then she added: "Why will you not realize, Chloé, what I am trying to do for you? Bion has already spoken to his brother who is a freedman. He is willing to buy you and make you his wife. Then you would be safe. If he comes down here and finds you playing with a young Roman he will have none of you."

Chloé had taken this arranged marriage with Bion's brother for granted. Now it was suddenly horrible torture to her—as terrible as the thought of Geta.

"Bion's brother is old and grey and ugly. He shall not touch me. He shall not!" she cried.

On the tenth day Melissa said:

"I do not doubt but that the young man has gone back to Rome."

Chloé stamped her foot.

"He will never go back to Rome. Never," she retorted.

But Melissa had at last broken her faith. Even Melissa by the next day wished she had not. For Chloé began to cry softly and continually. She worked blindly through her tears. In the late afternoon she would steal secretly over the forest path to the garden and look for him over the wall. This was while Aulus was at Sulmona. The villa certainly looked deserted. And the horses wandered in the pasture; all but his special horse which he took on long journeys. Yes, he was gone to Rome.

The Sulmona case completed and won, Aulus's first thought was to tell Chloé. He returned in late afternoon; but he went to the hut without changing his cloak. He came up noiselessly, or perhaps the sound of the blowing wind hid his steps. Anyway, he came quite up to the loom before Chloé heard him. She turned with a smothered cry, covered her face with her hands, and began to sob passionately.

"Oh, what is it? What has happened to you?" Aulus asked.

But she ran into the hut to hide her tears.

"She has had something to make her anxious. She'll be all right in a moment," said Melissa vaguely.

Aulus's first thought was that some slave had been about, frightening her, hurting her. He was beside himself with anxiety.

"Come out, Chloé, please come out and tell me," he called.

At last she came out to him. He took her hand and led her to the forest place by the brook. He was blaming himself bitterly for leaving her unprotected. He was frightened.

"Tell me, dear child," he said when they were alone. "Don't be afraid to tell me what has hap-

pened. I will care—I will care," he added wonder-
ingly, "as if it had happened to myself."

But she bowed her head as if in shame, and no
answer came from her.

"Can't you see I am frightened!" he said almost
angrily. "I have the right to know."

Then she looked up and said with distant dignity,
"Oh, nobody has been here to hurt me. Bion protects us."

"Why Bion?" he thought. A glimmer of the truth
came to him.

"Are you angry with *me*, Chloé?"

After a pause:

"No, not now."

Then he made the leap.

"But surely it is not because I was away? I went
to Sulmona to try a case."

"Melissa said you had gone to Rome."

So that was the trouble! He had gone away without notice. Chloé cared to this extent. She was white,
no color now. Her eyes were swollen with weeping.
He had become necessary to her. He had made these
visits to the hut without thought of the harm they
might do her—he who was planning to do her only
good. Now—yes, the child was in love with him. He
had been pretending all this while that she was a
child. He knew perfectly well that she was not. She
was a woman, with a woman's emotions, and she was
in love with him.

Aulus was so startled that he stood awkwardly

still. The knowledge gave him no pleasure—far from it. This was very complicated and troublesome.

"I must go," said Chloé hastily. "It is time to fetch the goats."

"I'll go with you," he said, but she showed no pleasure. All the way up the hill she said never a word. All her sweet unconsciousness of self was gone—gone. He tried to talk to her, but she answered in monosyllables.

"Are you angry with me?" he asked again.

She shook her head. He was aware she could not answer for some secret emotion. This was dreadful indeed. Once, as they came down with the goats, she stumbled and he caught her. A strange thrill went through him—a rush from realms of mystery, as if some god had warned him. Aulus did not believe in the gods, but what was more important, he had forgotten *not* to believe in them.

They came down to the hut. Chloé at once hurried to the milking. She seemed glad of any excuse to get away from him. He was hurt at this. He said good-bye and went away.

CHAPTER 24

And Somewhat a God Shall Give Thee

Thou shalt bethink thee somewhat in thine own heart and somewhat a god shall give thee.

The Odyssey

Mightily disturbed was Aulus all the way home. He had done Chloé infinite harm. This in return for her saving of his life, and for Melissa's saving of his arm. He had found Chloé at peace; he had now filled her with sorrow. If he kept on visiting her she would grow worse; if he stopped visiting she would suffer and be humiliated. He had thought so grandly of freeing her from slavery—now he had put upon her a slavery to sorrow. What a fool he had been! What a fool not to see it before! He realized that his very sense of superiority over her had made him blind. Well, he would go there no more. But, by Pollux, he would find some way to buy her freedom. Perhaps Cornelia would help him. As a slave, Chloé had no protection whatever. How that had frightened him, that first thought that harm had come to her!

He came to his room, began to put away in neat Roman order the papers of the Sulmona case and the law scrolls. He recalled that moment in his oration when he had driven home the victory, and the cruel usurer had fairly shrunk down in his seat. Then, at the end, the happiness of the farmer, secure at last of his home. Aulus could tell all that to Chloé. She was quicker than anybody he knew to see a point. He would——

Suddenly, like a clash of cymbals, came the thought that he was not going to the hut again. He would not tell his news or anything else to Chloé. This was painful. A blankness came over him: the kind of feeling he used to have on awakening during the winter when he remembered he was banished. He went on arranging his papers, muttering, "Fool—fool!"

He ate hardly any supper; went to bed early and to sleep.

He awoke suddenly in the night as if by a summons. He awoke in a clearness of mind in which all confusions were adjusted. As saith Homer:

"Thou shalt bethink thee somewhat in thine own heart and somewhat a god shall give thee."

He saw himself as going back to Rome, into the old life, winning office in the Forum, fame in the field, meeting his father again, being betrothed to some wealthy girl—that stoutish one who lived just beyond Lævinus, she was the most likely one. Life at its Roman best, and the whole thing was dead as last year's grave.

Why had he thought he could exist in that way apart from Chloé? Why had he not seen that all happiness, all vision, all that made life moving and sweet, were in her? He saw in this clearness, this new clearness, all she had done for him. Pulled him out of the pit? That was nothing. She had pulled him out of the pit that was himself, out of loneliness and weariness of life. She had pulled him up into warmth and sunshine which he had not known existed. Chloé! All her sweetness, delicacy, wit, her ardor of loving, each one of these walked like a separate light into his consciousness, and in so walking thrilled and shook him, and alarmed his whole nature with joy. And each time she came, his whole nature answered to bless her.

He did not think of practicalities, whether she was a slave, or Lævinus's rightful daughter, or how he would make her his wife. But he knew that he would make her so, in face of his father's anger, in face of Fate. Honorableness and Chloé had dwelt together in his mind from the first. They were not severed now.

He was so happy that he could not sleep again. He lay motionless in that clear consciousness and knowledge of joy until the morning. He breakfasted, and as soon as might be, hurried through the dew-drenched forest path to her hut.

"Where is Chloé?" he asked Melissa, startled to see Chloé's empty loom.

"She is down by the stream, washing wool," said Melissa. "Why in the world does he run so fast?" she thought, as Aulus hurried away.

He came to the waterfall. Below, where the fall found a pool, he saw her, dear and beautiful, spreading the fluffy whiteness of the washed wool upon the grass. It might have been white clouds and she the cloud spirit in charge of them.

"Chloé!" he called.

She looked up, wondering.

"Chloé, come here to me."

She rose from her knees, began climbing the rocks with that swift fawn-like sureness that was hers. All his life Aulus was to remember like sight each move of that dear approach.

"What has happened?" she asked, for announcement was in his face.

"Chloé," he demanded, "do you love me?"

She hesitated a moment. She had been so ashamed yesterday. But she was not ashamed now.

"Yes," she answered.

"Tell me how you love me."

Even to this she replied readily, as though released in a dream.

"I love you as the sight of my eyes, and more than life."

He drew her swiftly to him and with his hand turned her face up toward his, so she must gaze straight forward.

"And now hear how I love you," he told her. "As the sight of my eyes and more than life—more than life——"

Suddenly he dropped the play and was kissing her, holding her so close that she seemed shut into some golden world, safe and still. It was as if they sensed some vast harmony of which they were a part, into

which no adverse will could break. They did not
know how long they stood there.

"And yesterday you thought I did not love you!"
Aulus said in that new voice he had now.

"Yes."

"Some of us were very foolish. But now we are
wise."

"I have been wise a long while," Chloé boasted.

"How long?"

"Ever since I saw you riding the horses."

"Are you trying to tell me that you loved me even
before you helped me out of the pit?"

"I am not *trying,* I am *telling* you. It was because
I loved you that I leaped in beside you. I could not
bear for you to be alone in that dark."

"And I was angry! Do the gods ever forgive fools?"

"They would have to forgive you if they looked
upon you!" asserted Chloé with infinite admiring.

The spray from the waterfall blew with a sudden
gust over them—spray startlingly cold. Aulus laughed.
But Chloé said:

"It is the nymph. She gives us her lustration."

And Aulus had no wish to deny it.

Melissa called Chloé in the silence.

"We will go now and tell her," said Aulus proudly.

"But she will be angry." Chloé shrank from any
jarring upon this joy.

"Not with what I shall tell her," Aulus said.

So Melissa, working at her loom, was amazed to
see them coming, step by step—so close together,
bringing as it were a gift.

"Yes," Aulus answered the look. "We are as you see us. And Chloé is to be my wife."

"Oh, the very words of Lævinus!" thought Melissa, tragically holding her peace.

"It is easier for me," said Aulus, "because I am banished. That leaves me more free. But I shall write to Cornelia today. She is my friend because I tried to save her son, Tiberius Gracchus, and she will do much for me. I am asking her to come down to the villa and to see Chloé and to give me sanction of marriage. And I think my father will regard her word."

Melissa's face softened. Ah, this was different. Aulus was indeed doing everything in his power. Marriage counted for naught without such sanction of the elders. In Rome it was entirely in the elders' hands.

"But first I shall buy you and Chloé," Aulus went on. "Cornelia will give me the money. Then I will free you both."

Melissa gave a little gasp of wonder.

"I do not consider you slaves, either of you. Chloé, especially, is the daughter of Lævinus." Chloé started, for Aulus had not spoken of this before. "But I shall put you both beyond any tripping of the law. Manumission will do that."

Tears began to steal down Melissa's cheeks. The long disgrace of years—to be lifted, to be lifted!

Then Aulus, his speech finished, leaned toward Melissa and kissed her.

After this the whole friendship was to begin over again. Aulus wanted to tell Chloé everything about his family to which now she would belong, their health, their high standing in Rome. Of his father with his dour severity; of his mother, who would have loved Chloé so dear; Gnæus, who was still Aulus's enemy, and was the family's one disgrace.

"Gnæus is betrothed to Lavinia. Do you know about her? She is your sister."

"I know that she exists," said Chloé bitterly. "Are we alike?"

"Not one feature!" declared Aulus. "Not one. But," studying Chloé keenly, "you do look like your brother Kæso. He might be your own instead of half-brother. Yes, astonishingly like."

"He wears the tunics that I weave. Even his *toga virilis* was my weaving—yet I have never seen his face. And he to see mine would be ashamed." Chloé's face flushed with slow anger.

"Not when you are my wife, Chloé," said Aulus kindly.

He told her about Cornelia and how continually kind she had been to him.

"Cornelia is sure to understand us and be wise," he said.

But Chloé was afraid of Cornelia, afraid to be judged by her.

Then Aulus told Chloé the story of the great love that had existed between Cornelia and her husband, Gracchus. Gracchus had found two vipers in his room, an omen which the soothsayers reported as meaning the death of Gracchus or else of Cornelia within the year. If Gracchus released the male snake, he himself would live; if the female, Cornelia would survive. But Gracchus so loved Cornelia that he killed the viper which meant himself, preferring to die in Cornelia's stead.

"I'm beginning to think all such omens are nonsense," said Aulus wisely. "But the fact remains that Gracchus loved Cornelia better than his life. Do you not think that a woman so beloved will be tender toward another who is loved as well?"

And so Chloé plucked up courage to meet the great Roman lady.

Aulus planned that they should live, all three of them, in the Villa Cornelia. Even in spite of the talk it would make among the slaves, he led Chloé and Melissa down the hill across the horse pasture and into the quiet house. He led them through the rooms which were to be their home.

In all this Aulus was fair and frank and just. So they waited, steeped in happiness, for Cornelia to come to them.

CHAPTER 25

Splendid News

The letter from Cornelia did not arrive. But instead came another letter, utterly surprising, from Aulus's father. It was brought by a special messenger. Publius Cornelius had returned to Rome. Instead of being angry with his son Aulus, he was overwhelmingly pleased. The letter ran:

"You fought bravely in the Forum to save Tiberius Gracchus, one of the finest men of Rome. In all the matter of the land laws, you held yourself upright and just. I at last have a son of whom I can be proud—who can carry on the family name. I have seen the senators in power, and your banishment is rescinded. You can return to Rome at once. As I am working to secure you a public office, the sooner you get here the better. Besides all this, the death of Verania is a great grief to me. I wish to see you."

Aulus was touched as he never expected to be by anything from his father. He knew enough of the stern old warrior to realize that this letter meant affection, dependence, and a terrible impatience to see him. Life and career were made for Aulus. And as for Chloé, his father in this mood might grant him anything. Cornelia would help in that. Chloé would be his wife, not remotely here in the moun-

tains, but in Rome. Aulus was not naturally a country man. Oratory, the stirring public life of Rome,
these were his bent. Yes, life, so niggardly for a
while, was suddenly holding out both hands full of
gifts.

He wasted not a moment. He hurried to Chloé
with the news. She was not at the hut, but had
gone down to the villa for wool, bringing Melissa's
supply as well as her own. He hurried down the
hill.

He met her halfway. She was toiling up the hill
with the double burden. The wool even in the basket
was hot against her back. She was thinking: "Oh,
Slavery! Burdens! Soon I shall be free of you. Aulus
will save me," but even with such self-encourage-
ment she was exhausted.

Aulus came suddenly. He lifted the basket down
to the ground.

"Chloé, wonderful news! I have a letter from my
father."

"Not from Cornelia?" she inquired.

"No, no. It is, beyond hope, better. My banishment is lifted. I am free to go back to Rome."

Her face went as white as the wool.

"But you are not going?"

"Yes—yes, of course I shall go. Then I will send
for you."

"You said you would never go to Rome." Her
voice was hollow, strangely dead.

"No, Chloé, I never said such a thing."

"You acted it. I was the more deceived."

"I never deceived you, Chloé—never consciously by word or act."

The word hurt him as he had never been hurt before. He had tried with every faculty he possessed to be honest with Chloé.

"Please do not go to Rome," she said pleadingly, like a frightened child.

"But I *must* go. It would be unthinkable not to go when my father has sent for me."

Chloé, bred in her lonely hut, had no conception of family feeling, the strength of that sacred bond as it was in Rome. Their two minds stood facing each other at an impasse.

"When do you think you will come back?" she asked. The question confused him.

"I do not know, Chloé. I shall be under my father's authority." It did not occur to Aulus to lie to her. It would have been almost better if he had.

"But—— Oh, don't look so, Chloé! My father is suddenly kind to me. If I go quickly I can persuade him of our marriage. He will give me almost anything. Cornelia will be back of me."

"Yes, every stone must be moved to make them let you marry a slave."

"Chloé! How can you speak to me like that?"

For all her unreason, Chloé was in a way right. The chances against their marriage were great, and were made greater by this news. Suddenly she threw both arms about his neck in passionate entreaty.

"Do not go to Rome! Do not go to Rome! If you do I shall never see you again."

He kissed her tenderly. "Dear heart, don't you know I would come back if they tried to kill me?"

"Do not go. I will die if you go."

Aulus could not understand such unreason, such distrust. Besides—his whole career was at stake, and Chloé had not once thought of it. She seemed selfish, strange—a new Chloé. He tried to reason quietly with her, to explain the importance of this visit for his whole future life; but Chloé did not seem to grasp his meaning, only begged him over and over again not to go.

Aulus could not know that he was wrestling, not with flesh and blood, but with "principalities and powers." The hatred of Lævinus which had begun in Chloé almost before she could speak, which had been rampant in her childhood when Davus had beaten her, was in these last years dormant. But it was there, a poison to poison her whole mind. That the hatred was justified made no difference. Its harm was the same. It warped her judgment, filled her with fear. Rome—the going to Rome—was like a veritable curse through which all her life had been cursed. She could think of it in no other way. The wonder was that she had been able to trust a Roman even for a while. Only her deep love for Aulus had conquered. But now distrust, all Melissa's distrust and warnings—ah, they overwhelmed her! The hatred of Lævinus was like a coiled snake in her heart; and now it rose to strike the one she loved best in the world.

"If you go you will be like Lævinus. You will never come back," she said shrilly.

Now Aulus despised Lævinus. And especially he despised his treachery to Chloé's mother.

"How dare you compare me to him!" he said. "How dare you!"

"Oh, Melissa warned me and I would not hear, I would not hear." Chloé was shut now in her horrible world of hatred, talking to herself.

"Do you trust Melissa rather than me?" he demanded, but she hardly heard his voice.

"Oh, I am fortunate that you go before you pretended to marry me. So I will not be like my mother —I will die, but not as she died."

This was the last. Aulus's wrath, which was slow, slow to rise, rose at this. The kind of wrath which does not cease when once begun. He pushed her from him. That she was being ill-bred, like a slave, was as terrible to him as her cruelty.

"I thought I had had the greatest griefs life could give me. And now you have given me a greater. You—oh, that *you* should do it! I can never look upon you again."

Before he had finished he had dashed past her and was hurrying down the hill. Anywhere to get away from her. Chloé stood in dazed horror for a moment, then ran and stumbled like a hunted creature up, up to the hut. She broke in upon Melissa at her peaceful work.

"Oh, Melissa—he has gone to Rome. And I almost killed him."

She fell in a heap before Melissa.

"Oh, I was cruel—I was made of cruel words. And I said them to him—to him."

"Chloé, are you mad?" Melissa pulled Chloé to her feet. "Whom are you talking about?"

"Aulus, Aulus, Aulus. Oh, my darling, I have killed you."

Poor Melissa was frightened almost out of her wits. Chloé began to sob and cry so she could not speak. It was only gradually that Melissa learned that Chloé had not actually stabbed Aulus—but had only said wild words.

"I thought he was like Lævinus. Oh, I almost thought he *was* Lævinus!" she shuddered.

Melissa had some dim sense of what the mischief was.

"You should not think of Lævinus that way," she admonished.

"How could I think of him any other way?" Chloé said, white and rigid of face.

Melissa knew she must act quickly. She rushed off down the path Aulus had always taken toward the garden. Perhaps she could catch him. Oh, if he could only be made to understand—to forgive!

She was just in time, looking down into the horse pasture, to see Aulus gallop madly away, his slave following on a pack horse with the baggage.

CHAPTER 26

The Fortunes of Slavery

There followed days of tragedy. Chloé could neither eat nor sleep, but sat in dumb despair, unable to work. Melissa was afraid she would go into the kind of illness she had had after Davus whipped her—and so die.

"Aulus will never forgive me," she said over and over again. "He ought never to forgive me. I said unforgivable things. And I thought they were true."

She wished bitterly that she could write. If she could get a letter to him, she could unsay all those dreadful words. Not that he would forgive her at that, but that he should know that the words were untrue in her mind and so might forget them.

In the night the sentences would burn in her mind as if she were saying them over again. She seemed not to feel her own feeling in saying them, but Aulus's pain in receiving them—as if she were within his soul and knew. If she slept she would waken herself reciting the sentences aloud.

She wondered if she could send any message to Aulus by Bion. How disgraceful to have to confess those words to Bion, yet she would do it if it would clean them out of Aulus's mind and heart. But Bion was away at Rome now. And he was staying much longer than usual. So the weeks dragged on.

Of course Aulus did not return. That she did not for one moment expect.

Chloé might have died, might have gone mad, but she did neither. There came into her life a shock, which, dreadful as it was, saved her from these worse evils. Bion did not return. There arrived in his stead a new vilicus named Battarus. Bion, much prized by Lævinus, was needed in Rome. Battarus was a new slave, highly recommended for efficiency (the word and the quality itself were Roman), and he came prepared to make good. He would reorganize the farm from the foundation, make everything, especially the slaves, produce as much as they possibly could. He would economize materials, space, time— everything. Even Robina was afraid of him. He was not cruel like Davus, only cold and efficient. He came up to the hut, looked everything over with a fishy eye while Melissa and Chloé trembled. "Very neat hut, very neat outfit." Next day he made his decision. He saw no reason why two slave women should be separated from the rest, thus losing time in going and coming, and his own time in overseeing their work. He saw no reason why they should have a separate flock, when these could be cared for by the general shepherds. He commanded his assistant to drive the flock down the hill at once. Chloé and Melissa should finish the work they were doing, and their present supply of wool, then they were to move down to the slave quarters with the others.

He looked at Chloé.

"Is this the slave girl Geta was speaking of?" he asked one of his men, as though Chloé could not hear.

"Yes, sir."

"She is certainly old enough to be married. Geta should have a wife."

So he went—he and his men.

The two women stood as though lightning had struck them and burnt up all. They could see their flock going slowly down the hill. Only Psappha remained because she was old and blind and useless. Melissa sank to the ground. Life had had too many of these surprises. She had no plan, no resistance. Chloé stood rigidly still. Her lips were murmuring: "I won't marry Geta. I won't belong to Geta." And somehow she did not for one moment believe that that would happen to her. She belonged to Aulus. It made no difference that she had thrown away all the happiness. The "belonging" was the same and would always be the same. Even if Aulus did not want her himself, he would not want Geta to have her. She somehow had faith that Aulus still cared about her that much. It would be a further humiliation to Aulus, whom she had humiliated so cruelly already. No, she was sacrosanct for Aulus's sake. She began to stir restlessly, putting things together as if preparing for something. She did not yet know what. A thought seemed approaching from a long way off. A thought—a plan. Suddenly it was there, clear, swiftly completing itself in details.

"Melissa," she said. She went and put both arms about her, she now the mother and Melissa the child. "Listen to what I say. We are not going down to the slave quarters. I am not to belong to Geta. None of that is to happen."

Melissa looked up as if dumbly asking why.

"Because we are going to run away. Tonight we will do it. We will go early, in case Geta should come."

"They will catch us," said Melissa.

"If they do—it will make no difference. We will run away again. But I don't think they will. Even if Geta should come and find us away, he would think we were gathering wood. If he does not come, no one will know for a week. We will hide this afternoon in the forest. Then at night we will go down to Aulus's horse road on the farther side of the hill and go away so. We will drink all the milk we have in the bowls before we go, and we will take all our cheese and honey."

"What will we do when all that is eaten?"

"If we starve, it will be best," Chloé answered.

Chloé began to prepare for the journey. The activity made a strange relief, balking the thoughts which had stabbed her mind continually. Melissa had woven a long cloak, or cape, from the wool of their own sheep. She had dyed it dark blue. This had always been kept hidden from the slaves for fear of their jealousy, but it made a grand defense against the cold at night, Melissa and Chloé creeping beneath it together.

"Melissa will wear this," Chloé decided, laying it aside.

Melissa, beginning to waken as from lethargy, picked up an old and almost hairless goatskin which had been her bed.

"I'll sew part of this into a bag to carry our cheeses." She set to work. Presently she asked:

"But whither will we go?"

"I know not, we will just go away," Chloé answered.

"I know whither I would like to go."

"To the gates of Death?" guessed Chloé. She had been thinking of that.

"No, to Lesbos."

"But, Melissa, we could not reach there."

"We came from there," said Melissa plaintively. She stitched on in silence with her large needle.

"It is not impossible, Chloé," she said. "I have planned it often and often. My father had a brother, so much younger that he was my age. He purchased a ship and took oil to Poseidonia. After a while he married in Poseidonia and lived there. If we could find him or any of his children, they would be faithful and send us in their ship to Lesbos."

"How could we reach Poseidonia? Isn't it across the sea?" Chloé left her work and stood close to Melissa.

"No, it is here in Italy. Only a little way beyond Neapolis. Bion has gone there when he shipped wool to foreign shores."

Chloé's face lighted as Melissa thought it would never light again.

"Lesbos," she repeated, "Lesbos! It is like going to a star. But we will try. We will start out and try."

This made the whole matter different. Not mere running of fugitive slaves, but a return to home. As the afternoon progressed, the preparation was finished, the cheeses, etc., packed in the bag, and all hidden in the hut lest someone should come. They worked at their looms also, lest someone should come and see them.

"No one will know you in the cloak," said Chloé in low voice. "But they would know me. I wish I could look different. It would be safer." She worked on, and sudden as light this further plan came to her.

"Melissa, oh, I shall be different, too. I shall be a boy. Everything is here as if Apollo had known and tried to help."

She meant an old tunic and toga of Lævinus's son Kæso, which had been returned to the villa after Kæso was done with them, to be ripped out and woven again into some cheap garment. Fortunately Melissa had ripped only one seam of the tunic. That could be quickly mended.

In the afternoon, as ill luck would have it, Robina came for a call. She found the two of them weaving as if in steady discouragement. She talked in whispers about the new vilicus.

"He is hateful," she said. "Nothing that I cook

for him is any better than anything else. I don't know what we're coming to."

"I wish we had Bion back," said Melissa. "He was a blessing to the farm."

"Indeed and he was. Geta says I'll like the new vilicus when I know him better. But I won't. But Geta and he are always talking together as if they were friends."

Evidently Geta had not told his mother of his plan for Chloé. There was always the faint indication, even to Melissa and Chloé, that while Robina liked Chloé for herself, she did not like her as a mate for her son. Oh, would Robina never go! They had to be so careful, and Robina was the shrewdest person on the farm. But at last when the sun was toward its setting she hurried off.

"I had the supper all ready before I left," she said. "But I just had to see you and talk *him* over."

Poor Robina! She would miss them. And they would miss her.

In the twilight they drank their milk—all of it. Chloé took the little Apollo tenderly from the altar.

"You must not mind," she whispered. "We need you." She wrapped him in soft linen and put him into the bag. Then she brought Melissa the shears.

"Oh, hurry, Melissa. You must cut my hair. Truly short, the way the boys wear it in Rome."

Melissa obediently set to work; the long black curls fell to the floor. Chloé felt her head—she had no mirror.

"Shorter," she commanded. "It must be shorter."

"But it will make you so ugly."

"The uglier the better," Chloé asserted.

Presently she stood up in her short tunic, a veritable boy. Chloé's beauty was not such as flares up to meet the eye. The wonder was that Geta admired her at all. It was rather something delicate, to be searched for and savored and then deeply enjoyed. She made a wholesome-looking boy.

She hid the hair in the bushes below the cliff. Even that clue she would not leave. Together they set the looms in their usual place, the wool baskets in the corner. Chloé ran to the goat cave where lay Psappha, old and alone. She knelt and threw her arms about the hairy neck.

"Forgive us, darling," she said. "We do not want to leave you, truly we do not. You will have all the grass you want. Oh, I hope Robina will care for you, for our sakes." Tears fell down her cheeks upon Psappha's head, who meanwhile chewed her cud contentedly.

Chloé hurried out. For a moment she and Melissa stood together gazing for the last time upon their home. Then the kind, concealing forest received them. They were gone.

Chloé led the way to the far edge of the wood where they could look down upon Aulus's horse road. Here they waited. As soon as it was night, they crept down the hill to the road and began their journey. There was no moon, but the sky was adust with stars, shining with that silvery mist which scientists today say comes not altogether from the stars themselves but from some diffused power or light between them.

Now that the actual moment had come for leaving the only spot where Aulus could ever find her, Chloé was cut to the quick. It was Aulus's road, the path of his goings and returns; and now every step increased the fatal distance between them. She almost stopped. Then came the cruel thought: "If I stay, go down to the slave quarters, and become Geta's slave wife, then the distance from Aulus will be greater than the whole world." So, dreaming bitterly, she plodded on, keeping her steps back to fit Melissa's slower ones. Suddenly Melissa shook her, and she realized that galloping hoofbeats were coming toward them, on the road. They both ran to the bushes. In a moment more Olipor came by, hurrying late to the Villa Cornelia. Of course he knew nothing of the two pairs of anxious eyes that watched him pass. They waited. Someone might be accompanying him at a distance. But when all stayed silent and starlit, they crept out. Chloé realized that she must discipline her mind not to think of Aulus, or they might be caught.

For an hour they walked on, two hours, three hours. Their road was only a rough mountain track. The farm people used night for sleeping. The two met no one. They carried the pack by turns, Chloé insisting upon the longer carry. As they reached Aufidena the light was beginning to dawn. Of course they did not enter the town, but hurried fearfully along, crossed the Sagrus River by a narrow shaky bridge, and found a road which led beneath the ancient cyclopean walls. It was Chloé's first town—the first she had seen in all her life—but she had no time, no inclination even, to wonder at it. Fortunately the road beyond began to mount the hills again. Daylight seemed to come by leaps upon them, and so many farms to pass. But presently a by-path led into the forest; this they took, going deeper and deeper, leaving the path itself for unbroken forest tangle. At last with golden sunrise filtering through the trees they sat down and ate their first meal. Then, spreading Melissa's cloak for a bed, they were soon asleep.

This was the best distance they made in their whole journey. Never again could Melissa go as fast. Indeed her steps slowed and slowed day by day, until Chloé was frantic trying to walk as slowly as she. They traveled by night. The third night was one of continuous thunderstorm. Chloé was not frightened. To be defenseless in the forest was not so different from being in the hut, when the hosts of storm marshaled and gave battle. She was only thankful that the delay had not occurred nearer home. After passing Æsernia, whose name they did not know, they lost their way, taking the mountain track toward Bovianum, instead of the downhill way to Teanum. Here they ate the last of their home food. "Now we are beggars," thought Chloé and for the first time fear crossed her and mingled with her grief.

CHAPTER 27

Poseidonia at Last

They must now travel by day. The country was very wild and uncultivated. The first farm at which they begged refused them. The second gave them so little that they were almost as hungry after eating as before. Both Chloé and Melissa were deeply humiliated by the experience. "It is no pretense," thought Chloé. "We really are beggars. Perhaps we will be so for years and years. I wonder what Lævinus would think if he knew."

One noon, on a lonely mountain track, they passed a band of rough men eating a meal. They were long-haired, clad in skins. One might almost expect them to have goat legs like fauns. At sight of the travelers one of them sprang up as if to run toward them. Melissa and Chloé were too frightened to stir. But his companions pulled him down again with loud laughter. Chloé could not imagine what it meant, save that they thought they could capture such slow travelers later at their leisure after the meal was finished. As soon as the two had passed a blessed curve of the path, they turned into the forest, climbing by a stream side. A poor ruse for escape, but the best they could practise. Sometimes they thought they were followed but could not tell. Such bands of men frequented the roads, capturing travelers and selling them as slaves.

Toward nightfall they passed over the mountain ridge and looked down upon a beautiful lake. In the green, hidden valley was a single farm, small with a high wall close about it as if for defense.

"We must beg there," said Chloé, "no matter what they do to us."

As they approached the wide-open gate, two dogs sprang out and attacked them. Chloé stood close to Melissa, hitting out with a stick, but in despair of really defending herself. But soon a boy ran out after them.

"Lie down, Guarder, you old fool, lie down, Trick," he shouted. "Fool dogs," he commented, "to go after travelers like you! We keep 'em for bandits. Who are you?" he demanded.

"We are Greeks from Neapolis," answered Chloé, "and we are trying to return there." This was what they had determined to tell.

"Greeks! Well, my father'll treat ye fine, then. He loves Greeks."

The boy led them through the small compound, crowded with goats, sheep, and chickens, and into the house. Even so rude a house was built about a primitive atrium with a hearth. The owner, a bearded shepherd, was sitting by the fire.

"Here are some Greeks, Father," said the boy. "Guarder nearly ate them up."

The man rose to welcome them.

"Night grows cold in the mountains," he said, "even by summer. We'll have supper in a minute."

The wife came in, hurrying to heat a great pot of stew; a lame slave moved about, waiting upon her. All were kind. It seemed almost unbelievable after such a depth of need. Presently Chloé noticed the man staring at Melissa, watching her. What did it mean, why did his manner so frighten her?

Suddenly the man said:

"Melissa!"

Chloé gave a low cry.

"How do you know me?" Melissa demanded.

"Don't you know me, Melissa?" the man returned her question. "Have I changed so much since Lesbos?"

Melissa sprang up. She came close, close to the man, searching his face. Then, with almost a moan, she threw both arms about his neck.

"Kleus, Kleus, Kleus!" she sobbed.

Even then Chloé did not know what it meant. She had forgotten the name of the Lesbian seaman who had saved the ship from wreck in the Ægean. Melissa had told her the story when she was such a little girl. Lævinus had not freed Kleus for this good deed. He brought him to the villa, but before the child Chloé's birth Kleus had escaped.

What an excitement was now in the shepherd's house, Kleus explaining to his wife who Melissa was.

"And this must be our Chloé's son," he said, taking Chloé's hand. "I remember there was a little boy baby. Ah, these are my own people. All we island folk are related."

He told Melissa how he had escaped from the villa, how he had come to this farm and hired himself as a shepherd.

"The farm had no young man, only the old one, then the daughter of the farm took a fancy to me and we were married. So I have come to own the farm."

Melissa in her turn told of the new vilicus, and how she and Chloé had run away, and how they hoped to meet her uncle in Poseidonia.

"I've been to Poseidonia," said Kleus, "shipping wool from there. And I heard of that Lesbian man. I did not meet him, but I know he is there."

All this was wonderful news. Melissa and Chloé could hardly believe this sudden security and peace. Melissa hoped that they might even remain at the farm, but Kleus's wife seemed not to share this wish, and her word was law. Kleus had not won complete freedom when he came to own the farm! So after a few days the wayfarers knew they must go onward.

Chloé was not sorry. The leisure made her miss Aulus and long intensely for him. She spent the time amusing the little ones, telling them stories as well as she could in the Oscan language which was the speech of these mountains. Kleus had children little and big. The boy Pheres who had saved them from the dogs made a special companion of Chloé— "Lades," as he was told to call her; begging her to run races with him and to play ball. Lades made a creditable boy comrade. Pheres was several years younger.

But soon the visit was over. Rested, and with food in their goatskin bag, Melissa and Chloé resumed their journey. Pheres guided them over the Tifernus Mountains to where a clear track led down to Teanum. There he said a regretful good-bye.

As they neared Teanum, but still on the height, Melissa suddenly shook Chloé's arm.

"*Thalassa,* oh, *thalassa!*" she cried. "The sea, the sea!"

It was the Greek's cry of love for his own. Chloé, looking, saw where the far horizon melted into violet haze—poetry and unreality. They sat down by the roadside to gaze at it. To Chloé it was the desire of a lifetime. Who shall say what the sea means to the island-born! They did not notice a traveler coming nearer and nearer on the road, walking breathlessly fast. They were startled out of their dream only when he was quite upon them and shouting,

"*Hola, hola*—both of you. I'm here! I'm going with you. No, nothing you can say makes any difference. I'm going to Poseidonia. I'm going to Lesbos. Yes, to Lesbos."

It was Pheres. He had lagged behind them all day and now revealed himself.

"But you cannot come," scolded Melissa. "It is just as if we were stealing you. That would be a rank unkindness for all Kleus has done for us."

"I hate the farm. And I won't go back. If you

will not let me walk with you, I'll walk just a stadium behind you all the way—I don't have to go with you. But I'm going."

Melissa begged, pleaded, even wept, but it made not the slightest impression upon Pheres.

"And I've brought Trick with me," he said jubilantly, as if all had been agreed upon. "He can perform tricks really."

Trick began to wag his tail, certain he had been brought into the conversation.

"Look!" went on Pheres. "You two are silly to beg. You don't have to. The way Lades can tell stories and act 'em! We can act along the road like the *circulators*. Melissa can tell fortunes, and Lades and I will act the stories, and Trick will sit on his hind legs and balance a nut on his nose. So we will be circulators."

"Oh, Melissa, that would help so much!" chimed in Chloé. The begging from door to door almost broke her heart.

Melissa allowed the boy to sleep near them in the wood. Next morning she did battle with him, and she and Chloé walked down to Teanum without him. But in the end Pheres won, following them mile after mile as he had threatened to do.

At Teanum they met the Via Latina, a smooth, broad way easy to walk. They were now in the Campania. Perhaps if there is any most beautiful vale on earth, this is it. Purple-lighted, with fields of flowers, orchards of grey olives, cliffs jutting out into a sea which seems lighted from within with deep-blue fire.

The beauty invaded Chloé's mind, thrusting back her grief which seemed to become a dull and distant ache while her eyes rejoiced. Pheres enlivened the way. He made them act even when it was not necessary—stories of Lesbos, stories of Thebes, stories from the Iliad.

At Capua they heard a report that an epidemic of fever was raging in Rome. It made Chloé anxious for Aulus. But she knew that the better people escaped Rome at such times. So she hoped that all was well. Capua was the largest city in Italy except Rome.

They acted in the agora. Trick was a great favorite, and the three won applause and obols as well.

The Via Latina passed not through Neapolis but several miles back of that city, and they followed the Via. They saw Vesuvius, then a harmless mountain which never in the history of man had emitted fire. They turned out of the Via into an age-worn road which led southward to the sea's edge, and so came at last to Poseidonia.

Chloé was not prepared for Poseidonia. Bion had told Melissa nothing about the city, and Melissa knew nothing save that long ago it had been one of the Greek cities of Magna Græca. But Poseidonia was a colony of Sybaris, of Dorian and Achæan blood. At this time it was five hundred years old. It had been twice conquered by the Lucanian barbarians, then it had been overcome and repopulated by Rome. One would think that no Greek touch could be left upon it.

The three strolling actors sought the main street of the town where they might perform for the crowd. Here Chloé stopped in bewilderment.

"Melissa," she whispered, "what am I seeing, am I in a dream? Have we come to Greece?"

There, beside the milling Roman street, stood three Greek temples, massive and of naked dignity. They were a blaze of color, yet not one glorious line of them was interrupted by any ornament. The central one was Poseidon's—as its pediment showed. Its huge Doric columns rose without base from the pavement, as if their strength would hold the vault of heaven. They held instead the level lintel and pure, dreaming roof. Repose was there, mystery, and a faith that, whatever its detail, rested in the great heart of God.

Chloé was moved as the Greek was ever moved by beauty. Not a mere appreciation but a shaking emotion like love or ecstasy. Chloé forgot that she was a beggar, a fugitive slave. She even seemed in that moment to drown all quarrel with Aulus in an elemental agreement.

"Let us go in, go in," she chanted. "We haven't a gift, but the god will receive us."

"My darling," said Melissa, "I cannot go one step more. I will sit here and rest while you and Pheres go. Perhaps I can tell a fortune and win an obol while I wait." So she sat down on a step of the temple platform while the two young creatures sped on toward the beauty which called them.

Within the *cella*, it was dim with lofty shadows. There were no Greek treasures, only some war trophies which the Romans had stored there, and the archaic statue of Poseidon in stark grandeur towering to the roof.

Chloé glanced back through the doorway to where Melissa sat in the brilliant sunshine. Then she faced the statue, lifted both hands on high and prayed:

"O Poseidon, give us a good and happy voyage to our dear isle. Apollo hath brought us thus far, do thou bring us farther."

Something made her glance back again through the door. A man was standing by Melissa, and in that moment he jerked Melissa to her feet and shook her. It was violent, menacing. Some dreadful thing was happening. Her first thought was that Pheres must have no part in it.

"Pheres," she whispered, "go closer and look at the shields while I run and fetch Melissa. She must not miss this."

Pheres obeyed, and Chloé flew like a swallow out of the *cella,* down the temple steps to where Melissa was.

"You do not know me," Melissa was asserting to the man. "You have nothing to do with me."

"Oh, yes, I do though. You were the best weaver on the farm. I know ye well enough."

Here Chloé ran up.

"Go away, young man," cried Melissa coldly. "You need not arrest me too."

Chloé knew well that Melissa was trying to deceive her captor and to free her from the trouble.

(Darling Melissa—her only friend in the world.) For answer she clasped Melissa's hand in her own.

"Now where'd ye spring up from?" said the man to Chloé. "Her son! Double luck, by Pollux!"

He whipped off his leather belt and tied Chloé's hands. With horror Chloé recognized him, though he did not recognize her. He was one of Davus's men— one of the guard that used to come up to the hut when Davus whipped her. A crowd was gathering.

"What's happened? What is it? Murder! Fugitive slaves, what?" they screamed in Latin, Oscan, Greek, a perfect clamor.

"Yes, it's runaway slaves," the man shouted. "I knew 'em in Samnium. I'll get a good price for 'em, too, if I take 'em back."

All the while he was pulling them along, trying to get away from the people who might put in a rival claim.

"We have kindred here," cried Chloé in the din. "Don't you dare to take us! Pitticus will help us. Pitticus will give reward."

"Yes, yes," said one in the crowd. "There is a Pitticus who lives here."

For a moment the man hesitated.

"Pitticus be damned!" he said. "I don't know him. But I know Lævinus, and I know that these are slaves and belong to him."

By this time he had got them off the main street into a lane. A donkey stood there. Melissa fell flat on the pavement. The man set her on her feet. But a few steps farther she fell again.

"Stop yer nonsense," he yelled. "Ye can walk well enough."

But presently he saw that she could not. The shock, the fright coming upon her great weariness, had made Melissa too weak to walk at all. He lifted her upon his donkey, setting her behind the pack, and held her erect with one arm while he gave the beast a cuff which set him going. Chloé, with her tied hands, hurried along beside. Thus dazed, blank with suffering, they passed out of the Roman gates of Poseidonia.

"By Pollux, this is a good day's work," rejoiced their keeper.

The man was a true product of the slavery system. He was not particularly cruel, nor was he outwardly cruel to Chloé and Melissa. But he thought no more of blasting their hopes, of haling them back to their owner, than he would think of catching two fish from the sea and selling them in the market.

CHAPTER 28

Katharsis

They arrived at the villa after but a five days' journeying, undoing so easily the distance which had taken the heroism of their whole hearts to traverse. A villa boy, seeing them at Aufidena, ran forward to tell the news. Robina met them at the edge of the estate. They were more dead than alive—Chloé white and staggering, weighing pounds less than she had weighed a month ago, Melissa in a faint, having to be held bodily on the donkey.

"Oh, Robina, Robina!" cried Chloé, throwing herself into Robina's arms. "Oh, what shall we do?"

"Baal have pity!" cried Robina, tears streaming down her face. "O Baal, save us!"

She gave Chloé a great hug, then turned to Melissa.

"She's goin' to die, sure, sure," was her way of comfort. "Here, lay her on the ground. Get me water, one of ye—don't stand there starin'," she addressed the curious slaves who had gathered about. "And fetch me that narrow bench in the kitchen. Ye kin carry her on that."

The water brought Melissa to, but not to full consciousness. She moaned in delirium—looked up wild-eyed, then suddenly closed her eyes again in utter exhaustion.

"Oh, Melissa, don't ye know me?" pleaded Robina. "Gods, but ye look awful! Oh, are ye goin' to die?"

"Hey, now!" interposed their keeper. "She mustn't do that. I've got to get some pay for all this fetchin' of her."

"Ye'll get your pay good and plenty when the vilicus comes back," Robina told him. "Ye don't have to bother about 'em now. I'll see to 'em."

Chloé sat by the roadside, too exhausted to help. Melissa die? She hoped she would. That would be escape for her. If only she could die with her!

Even the gods had deserted them. Had she not been in the very act of prayer to Poseidon when this cruel man had come upon them? As for what awaited them in the villa, she could not even approach that thought.

"Ye're lucky," Robina was saying to Chloé. "The new vilicus is off to Rome just now. He was mad as an eagle at yer gettin' away. And he whips as bad as Davus when once he begins."

Chloé hardly heard her.

"And ye shall go up to the hut," Robina added, "no matter what he says. There's no place for a sick woman in slave quarters. Here, you fellows, carry Melissa along."

She seized Chloé's hand and helped her to her feet. The men carried Melissa on the rude bench, and so painfully, they ascended the familiar path.

"How far did ye get?" queried Robina, with arm tenderly about Chloé.

"To Poseidonia."

"What? Why, that's a hundred stadia from here. Gods, but ye were clever. And we never knew when ye went. Nobody was up here for a week. But what queer clothes ye've got on!"

All the while Chloé was thinking, "Geta, Geta." But she dared not ask about him—lest asking would bring him sooner.

Almost everything had been stolen from the hut. Robina brought a blanket for Melissa to lie upon, helped Chloé to bathe her. She sent for food from the kitchen. Kindness, kindness, which seemed to push back for a while the dread fate that must await the two as runaway slaves when the vilicus returned.

Then suddenly a buxom young woman came panting up the hill, her mouth full of news.

"Oh, Robina, Robina," she called while yet on the lower cliff. "Come, quick, quick, quick! A messenger from the master. And he'll be here tonight."

"What are ye talkin' about?" queried Robina. "What master?"

"Oh, the master in Rome." By this time the girl was with them, and Robina shook her by the shoulders as if she were her own daughter.

"Ye're crazy. The master hasn't been here come eighteen years."

"But he's comin' now," the girl sobbed with fright. "There's a fever in Rome—a terrible plague. They say just everybody's died. Lævinus's whole family. Lævinus is runnin' away from it. He's almost to Aufidena. Oh, ye should see 'em down at the villa. All of them scared and cryin' and scrubbin' the atrium, fixin' the garden, trimmin' the hedges, and killin' a lamb. They say ye must cook the biggest dinner of your whole life!"

The news had pierced Robina's consciousness. She stopped not a moment for good-bye, but went running like a hurricane down the hill.

Chloé stood in the same spot as if stunned. Of all the terrible things that had happened to her in the last month this was the worst—that Lævinus should appear. It was as if her whole world had suddenly turned upside down. She tried to busy herself settling Melissa for the night, tidying the disordered hut, but she hardly knew what her hands were touching or doing. At last, worn out, she lay down on the floor beside Melissa and in spite of her excitement fell into a deep sleep.

She awoke at sunrise—the golden sun rays streaming into the door on the same old places. She had thought never to see the hut again. With returning consciousness the same strange excitement assailed her.

Lævinus! The man who had wrecked her life before it was begun, the man who had killed her mother by his desertion, who promised and performed not, the man whose image had peopled her dreams and her awakenings. There was in her a wild desire to see him, so that she found herself actually planning to run through the forest and watch behind the garden wall. That was the last thing in the world that she would really do. The only saving circumstance in the whole affair was that she was safely bestowed in the hidden hut, where surely he would never come. Lævinus, a terrible myth, a demon made of her thought! Now suddenly a Reality down there in the villa—probably eating his breakfast in the familiar atrium, walking in the garden—*her* garden, if anything in this world could be called hers, Lævinus, Lævinus! In spite of the pursuing thought, she bathed Melissa's face, gave her the simple breakfast. Melissa ate and went at once to sleep again—a sleep of exhaustion. Then Chloé went to her dear stream and bathed beneath the waterfall. She was refreshed in spite of having to put on again the old tunic in which she had traveled. She had no other. Robina had been shocked at her wearing a boy's garment. Chloé had sensed that yesterday. She tried to eat her breakfast but was too preoccupied, perhaps too frightened, to do so. There was nothing more to do. Even the wool had been stolen, so she could not weave. She sat down by the loom. She dreamed there for almost an hour.

She was aroused by a step on the path—Aulus's path, by which he always came through the forest. Aulus! Oh, could that be? Then Geta! At this thought she sprang up in fear. But it was neither Aulus nor Geta. It was a strange man with greying hair and an aspect of utter, beaten discouragement. In spite of the great change in him she knew him at once, she who had studied his portrait statue with bitter fascination. *It was Lævinus.* He was coming toward her. Oh, how in the name of all the Fates had he found the way hither?

"But he will not know me," raced her swift thought. "How could he possibly recognize me whom he has never seen?" Her heart was thudding like a runaway horse.

He came quite up to her before he lifted his head. Then, oh, what a terrible cry! He passed his hands over his eyes, he looked again.

"You are Kæso! You are Kæso! Oh, why do I see my dead boy everywhere!"

"What do you mean?" said Chloé coldly. "My name is not Kæso."

He lifted his trembling hands to his forehead.

"Of course not, of course not. Oh, I hope I am not going mad."

Then he did not walk onward, as Chloé prayed he might. He sat down as if wearied to death—the very ledge where Aulus always sat.

It was so strange, after seeing the calm white marble Lævinus all her life, now to see this human suffering person. She wished his hands would not tremble so. What right had he to suffer, he who had only caused suffering always? He must go away. She could not stand him so near. Should she run into the forest? But that would leave Melissa to his mercy. Oh, what should she do?

"You had better go on," she said rudely. "This is no place for you."

He seemed not to hear her as he kept murmuring to himself.

"Helvia dead. Lavinia dead. Kæso dead. If only one had been left! Only one!"

So that was what had happened—the plague. It had taken his whole household. The slave girl last night had said this, but Chloé had not noticed.

There was a horrid instant in which Chloé was glad. The avenging gods had come. They had visited Lævinus's sins upon him. They had swept away everything. He deserved it, he deserved it. The very atmosphere of Death seemed about him, Death which had struck so near. But, oh, why did he not seem more like what she had pictured? That would be easier than this. He seemed afraid to look at her; kept his head bowed. Now he was thinking of something else.

"I was a fool to come here to the villa," he said bitterly. "As if the years make any difference. In every room, in every corridor! It is only my dead Chloé."

Then Chloé's anger, horror, fear, all blazed into speech.

"How dare you say her name, when it was you, you, *you,* who killed her!"

"I kill Chloé? The very light of my life! All the light that was ever given me!"

"You did kill her. You went away and never sent her word. Then you married Helvia, and that killed her."

"I never did so. I would not marry Helvia while my wife lived, not if my father killed me."

How dared Lævinus deny these things, facts that were burnt into Chloé's soul? And now a change came over Lævinus. He was strong again, a very Roman, sitting straight and staring at her indignantly. Even so, Chloé was too beside herself with anger to be afraid.

"Is this what the slaves are saying here?" he demanded. "Even slaves shall not say it."

"But one slave does say it!" Chloé retorted. "One you made a slave when you had no right."

"Who told you this?" Lævinus went on wrathfully.

"Davus told it long ago."

"Davus was a liar from the beginning."

Chloé's world began to whirl into new shapes at the bare possibility that Davus had lied.

"And who are you who dare to question me like this?" Lævinus demanded masterfully. "Come here to me."

Chloé obeyed. As she neared him, such a desire to weep came upon her that she could not speak. But Lævinus, when she stood at his knee, forgot all his questioning and wrath. The same fearful longing came into his eyes meeting hers.

"Kæso, Kæso, feature for feature!" he said. He touched her tunic. "Great gods! It is Kæso's very dress, too. Here is a little rent at the neck. His pet dog made it in play. You've mended it—but it's there."

He paused in complete bewilderment. Then he

began softly to stroke her arm—lovingly, reverently.

"I suppose I am mad," he said. "But at least I have my son."

"I am not your son, I am your daughter!" Chloé burst out. It was the last thing in the world she meant to tell him. It swept out of her like divine truth.

"No," he said soothingly. "Do not confuse me. My daughter Lavinia is dead. You are not like her in the least."

"I am not Lavinia!" Chloé was somehow jealous of this sister. "I am not. I am Chloé."

But at the word "Chloé," Lævinus gazed at her with desperate searching. He must have seen some resemblance to his dead wife, for he turned suddenly white as death. His eyes went wild for an instant. Then he sank back against a ledge of rock. He was almost fainting.

Chloé ran to the stream for water. She was trembling so she could scarcely dip the bowl. It seemed as though she were clinging to her hatred for Lævinus with a clutch of desperation. She *must* hate him. She had hated him all her life. Her thoughts flew about like darting swallows. She must not be deceived. She must not let him deceive her because he was pitiful and full of grief. But he said, or he seemed to say, his father had coerced him. Perhaps, perhaps—oh, she must find out the truth! She must go slowly and find out the truth. It would be death to be deceived now.

She came hurrying back without pause, although

her emotions meanwhile had covered a world. Lævinus's eyes were still closed. She dashed the water in his face. She ran and fetched a small glass of wine which Robina had left for Melissa. This revived him.

He was sitting up now, watching her, observing her every movement with a keenness she could hardly bear.

"You are a kind child," he said. As she took the glass he seized her hand and gazed closely at it, from that to her face and back again to her hand.

"You are so strange—so strangely familiar." He dropped her hand.

"I had a touch of the plague when Kæso died," he confessed. "And—and I can hardly be right in my head now. It seems to me you said"—he paused, as if the word were too dear to pronounce—"that you are Chloé, and then you said you were my daughter."

Suddenly all the hatred that Chloé was clinging to fell out of her heart like a stone. It stopped like an old unbearable ache that had always been and now left her free. She was so weak that she sank to her knees. She longed to believe Lævinus—to believe him utterly—not to distrust at all. How could he have been faithless to her mother, he who pronounced her name like that, who looked at herself as he was looking now? Oh—suddenly all prudence flung itself to the winds. She *did trust him*. All the lies in the world could not touch her belief in him.

"You are my father," she said brokenly. "You are my father."

Lævinus seized her shoulders roughly. "What are you saying? Be careful. It makes all the difference between death and life to me. Death and life!" he repeated, leaning toward her again with that searching.

"You are my father," she repeated. "And Chloé was my mother. Oh, Father, it is true."

He was trembling now more than she, and very white.

"My brother said the child was dead and in Chloé's grave."

"Davus told him that," Chloé answered. "Melissa ran off into the woods with me, because she feared your brother would kill me."

"My brother would not have harmed you. It was I sent him to save you and Chloé. My father told Davus to sell Chloé and expose her child. That was the terrible fact. You must know it."

He was still holding her shoulders—a grasp that hurt. Then his face changed as belief dawned in it, and a tenderness Chloé never dreamed of. He drew her toward him close in his arms.

"Chloé's child, my child!" he murmured. "It is too good, too good to be true."

She could hear him breathing heavily. His arms were strong, he did not hold her clingingly as Aulus had held her, but with the very safety of fatherhood. Oh, how could she be so happy when Aulus was not here? But this brought her closer to Aulus, too.

It brought her closer to everything. To the gods themselves. Suddenly she realized that this was Lævinus who was doing this. Lævinus, the hateful Roman.

"Father, Father," she sobbed. "I have hated you. I hated you without a cause."

"Did you?" he asked. "Well, you shall love me *with* cause. With all the causes that I can bring to pass."

After a while he said:

"And you must love me, Chloé my daughter, because you are all I have in the world. All—all were taken away, and now you are given."

To be so precious, so desired—when she had thought she was cast aside and despised as a dog might be!

"Were you a slave?" he asked. "Did you live in this wretched hut?"

"Yes," she answered.

"You must have suffered—suffered much."

But they were too happy, too awed to explain and tell details. Chloé went into the hut and awoke Melissa, who was still sleeping heavily. Melissa listened, dazed, to Chloé's strange words. She was too weak to argue or disbelieve.

"It must be as you think, child," she said.

After a while a slave came hurrying, frightened at Lævinus's long absence, frightened now to see him sitting hand in hand with a poor shepherd boy.

It was Bion. Bion himself who had come to the villa with his master.

"No, Bion." Lævinus smiled at Bion's confused

expression. "I am not dead or mad. I have found a daughter. Haven't you known her all this while?"

"Yes, I have indeed. I was only deceived for a moment by her short hair and tunic."

"Oh, why did you not tell me?"

"I did not know—did not know—what to do."

"Bion saved my life," said Chloé.

"Yes, Bion would do that," said Lævinus affectionately. "Whom does she look like?" he demanded, proudly regarding Chloé.

"She is the image of you, master," said Bion.

"I never thought of such a thing," said Lævinus—very proud again.

"Well, master, look at her and you'll see yourself," said Bion.

But Bion all this while was looking anxiously about. His mind was not upon Lævinus or upon Chloé.

"Where is Melissa? I heard she is ill."

"Yes," said Chloé and led him into the hut.

There, to Chloé's astonishment, Bion fell on his knees beside Melissa, clasping both her hands.

"Oh, Melissa, Melissa," he said, "I will never leave you again."

And Melissa's thin cheeks flushed faintly with joy.

"He was dreadful. The terrible vilicus. Save us from him," she faltered.

"Yes, I will save you. Lævinus will give me what I want. He kept me in Rome away from you. But now you must be my wife so he will never do it again. I will save you, Melissa." Bion said this so fondly that Chloé realized that neither of them knew she was in the hut. She stole softly out, leaving them together.

Of course Chloé would not go to the villa without Melissa. So Bion was sent hastily for a litter and two slaves to carry her. He brought Melissa out in his arms and laid her upon the litter.

Presently they were going—Melissa borne on the litter ahead of them, Bion walking at her side, Lævinus and Chloé together. Away from the hut, away from slavery, away from suffering into the new unbelievable life.

Chloé felt so light, it seemed as if her body had no weight at all, that her feet had no need of the ground to tread on. She was free—not of slavery only, but of that hatred that was part fear, the fear that was all hatred—the hatred of Lævinus. She was suddenly realizing that this had taken an enormous energy to maintain—now that energy flew free in an effortless empyrean.

Could this be the same path up which Robina had helped her yesterday? Even the leaves of the smallest plant beside it looked different, even the trees looked different.

In Delphi was a place where Apollo purified men of unintentioned wrong. An elaborate ritual in the temple, the wise comforting of priests accomplished this. *Katharsis,* they called it. But Chloé had katharsis from a deeper source than even Apollo could give. Katharsis from a hatred she had harbored all her life.

CHAPTER 29

The Villa Garden

And now how wonderful it was to experience all the lesser joys which crowded about the greater, like good spirits about a central sun: to come to the villa and hear her father's formal welcome; to enter her mother Chloé's room, now her very own; to have brought from the villa storeroom a delicate white *stola* for her wearing, she who had worn only torn and coarse garments, though she wove so skillfully for others; to have the good food to give to Melissa, whose room was next to hers; to see Melissa grow strong and awake in the new happiness; then at last to sit at the evening meal in the garden, she on one side the table, her father on the other, the golden sun at setting and the cool evening breeze stirring her hair. Chloé, who had no table manners whatever, sprang up from her place, ran around to her father and kissed him.

"And why did you do that?" he queried, greatly pleased.

"To make up for all the wrong I did to you."

"And how shall I make up for the wrong to you, dear child, who had to be a slave so long?"

He kept her hand, detaining her. "It is almost as

if your mother were here again. Your presence brings hers. We will sacrifice to her spirit tonight.

"And," he added with Roman piety, "we will sacrifice also to the spirit of Kæso, to Helvia and Lavinia. My dear, your life would have been richer if they had been spared to us. Kæso was my hope and my companion; Helvia never disobeyed me in her life. Even little Lavinia had her place in my heart."

Robina, who never was required to wait upon the table, came in again and again on fictitious errands. She twitched Chloé's dress as she passed her to see if Chloé would smile or be proud.

"Oh, Robina, aren't you glad, too?" asked Chloé fondly. "Melissa is getting well again."

It was like a dream that she should be sitting so grandly and the mighty Robina waiting upon her.

Very clear now were the mistakes and deceptions of the years. Lævinus's father had indeed held him in Rome that time so long ago when he had thought only to stay a week. Old Marcus Lævinus had returned home suddenly from Spain, learned of his son's infatuation for a Greek slave, and determined to break it up at all costs. Marcus was a Roman father of the old school who not only had the life-and-death right over his son but proposed to use it. *Pater-potestas* was a fundamental law of Rome. He could see nothing in Lævinus's Chloé but a foreign woman of the worst sort. He held Lævinus in Rome by physical force, he intercepted his letters, he betrothed him to Helvia, and when Lævinus refused to marry her (for sons had the right of refusal),

Marcus sent Davus down to the farm to sell Chloé as a slave and expose her child. Lævinus was beside himself with anxiety and grief. He finally escaped his father's guard and ran away to the villa. He was halfway on the road when his father's men arrested him. Then Lævinus secretly sent his brother to the villa. The brother came back with the news that Chloé and her child were dead, he had seen the grave on the hill. After that Lævinus, thoroughly crushed, married Helvia and sailed for Egypt.

Davus, so it appeared, had been a good deal perturbed between the commands of old master and young master. Suppose the old man should die, then young master would kill or torture Davus for selling this woman and destroying a child of Lævinus's own. Thus it was that when Davus came to the villa he lied to Chloé about Lævinus's marriage with Helvia (for Lævinus was not yet married) and hid Chloé in the hut. Davus, so Lævinus guessed, had been disappointed and frightened when Chloé died. But he had determined to keep the child hidden for a possible reward. Then, years later when old Marcus died, Davus's unexpected manumission made him forget his villa schemes.

All this Lævinus had told his daughter in the afternoon.

"And now," he ended, "we will forget this. They are sorrows which even to speak of now are profound pain. You are my legal daughter and have been so all your life."

So they had sat down to their first meal together.

The relation of father and daughter in Rome was sometimes very beautiful. Men of great fame and worth, writers, orators, jurists, turned to their daughters for inspiration and companionship. Even the cruel warrior would with a daughter be all gentleness and persuasion.

After the meal Lævinus and Chloé walked in the garden.

"How old are you, *filia mia?*" he asked.

"I am seventeen."

"Oh, no, that is impossible! It cannot have been so long."

"Melissa says I am seventeen."

"And not married!" he exclaimed. "You are almost beyond the age. I must attend to that at once."

"I don't want to be married," said Chloé, frightened.

"Nor do I want you to be. How shall I bring myself to part with my daughter, even to the best young man in Rome? I cannot bear to let you go."

"Father, I don't want to be married," said Chloé again.

Suddenly a thought crossed Lævinus.

"Great Jupiter, you could marry my poor little Lavinia's betrothed. Then you would be only four doors away. Lavinia was betrothed to a son of Publius Cornelius. All the arrangements can be transferred."

"Lavinia's betrothed! Oh, no, no, no!"

He looked at her, saw she was white as cloth and trembling. He put his arm about her.

"My darling, I will never force you to marry. Would I visit upon you what gave me so much sorrow in my boyhood?"

Lævinus was anxious. He saw that this was no conventional hesitation. The child had had some terrible experience in her slavery.

"What has frightened you?" he said. "Tell me."

Chloé cowered in his arms. But it seemed impossible to tell her father about Aulus and the cruel words she had herself said to Aulus. How could he understand them when she did not understand them? How could she speak to anyone a thing so intimate and painful, when it was all mixed up with her hatred of Lævinus himself?

"I cannot," she faltered. "Not—now."

"Will you tell me, perhaps—some day?"

Chloé nodded.

Lævinus longed to know her secret trouble, but he knew he could never urge her. Parents who love their children must make such sacrifices—waiting for the young mind to come to theirs even if it never comes.

But the whole subject had brought Aulus to Chloé with sorrow and longing such as she had felt on the loneliest mountain road. She tried to throw them off. She must not grieve her father—him who had had such manifold griefs to bear. But all her spontaneity was gone. The lover's love overwhelms the father's even if it be so new-found a one and dear.

"I think you are very tired," said Lævinus. "Bion tells me you ran away from that substitute vilicus whom I sent to the farm and that you actually fled to Poseidonia."

"I do feel tired now," she confessed.

"And what gift would you like to have on this first night in your father's home?" he asked, still trying to divert her.

"I do want a gift," she said, brightening. "I have wanted to ask you ever since we came in at the villa gate."

"Well?" he smiled.

"It is an expensive gift."

"I will try to meet it."

"I want Melissa to be free. Oh, it does not seem right for me to be free and Melissa still a slave."

He was pleased at this. He thought everything Chloé did was like her mother.

"You shall have Melissa's freedom, not next week but tomorrow," he promised her.

So he kissed her good-night.

Lying in the strange soft bed, Chloé could think of nothing but Aulus. What right had she to happiness when she had caused Aulus such pain! Oh, if she could only touch his hand, see his face again! But how horrible it would be to be married to Gnæus and see Aulus coming in and out of the house when she might not touch or love him! Horrible, indeed! But Father said he would not do that if she hated it. Father was kind, kind! How strange and unaccustomed, this kindness and safety together!

Then wisdom came to her. She sat up in bed with

the instinct to run at once to Lævinus. But the house was still. She could hear the crickets chirping in the garden. Why had she thought she could not tell her father about Aulus? Of course she must tell him. Only so could she reach Aulus. Kind as Lævinus was, he would bear her message to Aulus, tell him that the words she had said were untrue in Chloé's mind —that she was unsaying them every hour—wiping them out. Forgive her—oh, but she must not hope for Aulus to do that. She had no right to hope. She would tell her father all—tomorrow morning early before breakfast. In the peace of this decision she fell asleep.

She awoke at dawn. She must have been dreaming of Aulus, for she awoke with bitter longing in her heart. She controlled it, tried to quiet it with the thought that soon she would be telling Lævinus about it. Soon the cruel words would be unsaid. But she could not lie quiet. She rose quickly. A slave whose duty it was brought water, hot and cold, for her to bathe. She dressed in the same long white *stola* and bound her hair with a coral-colored fillet of wool. Then she hurried out.

The garden was quiet and full of dreams. Dew lay everywhere, and the fine-wrought spider webs on the hedges were jeweled like coronets. Chloé wondered if the spiders had been worshiping Athena Spinner in the night. They were sacred to her. Aulus had said it was foolish to believe such things, but it was difficult for Chloé to disbelieve them. Aulus, Aulus, Aulus! How everything made her think of him! Was he safe? Might the Roman plague have caught him? Had he perhaps gone to another villa at Neapolis of which he had spoken? Where, where?

The golden light which had led the sun to his setting came with him now again this morning, pure and glassy clear as if it replaced the air with its own transparency through which one could almost see the trailing scarfs of the gods—the beyond-sights which mere air hides from our eyes.

Chloé paced up and down, waiting for her father, her long dewy shadow hurrying ahead of her or trailing behind her as she turned. There was the old break in the wall through which Aulus had always come. She loved it for letting him come through. She went there to look down—her old place for lingering. The futility of gazing into empty memories!

But the horse pasture was not empty. A horse stood there saddled, a groom, and—dared she believe it?—Aulus—there in the distant golden light—*Aulus* standing by the horse, making ready to ride away!

She thought only one thing. She would lose him! He was riding away. She leaped, in spite of her long *stola,* over the wall's scattered stones, she started down the hill. Then, fearing that she might not reach him in time, she whistled—a whistle, part of a bird tune, which Aulus had often used to announce his coming to the hut.

Aulus stopped, startled, his hand on the bridle. She whistled louder. Then he turned; saw her so distant and small on the hill. Would he stop? Would he ride away in anger? Her thoughts had hardly time to flash this before he dropped the bridle and came at a dead run up the hill. Coming to her, coming to her, only at the sound of a bird call. With a last leap he was there. He caught her to him, kissing her, holding her away to look into her face, kissing her again.

"Oh," she managed to falter, "you are not—— Oh, *are* you forgiving me?"

"I don't know," he laughed. "I only know I love you to distraction." Then: "How did you get here? I have searched everywhere for you. I was nearly mad."

"A man caught us at Poseidonia and haled us back," she answered.

"Blessed man! Some god instructed him."

A clearness crossed Chloé's mind. Poseidon of the great temple had answered her prayer beyond her praying. He had sent her back to Aulus's arms.

"Why did you run away?" he chided. "Didn't you know I would come back here to you?"

"It was a new vilicus. Oh, he was going to marry me to Geta—and I could only belong to you."

"So you ran away to save yourself for me. Poor little girl! I left you in such danger."

"It was my cruel words did it. They were all untrue. Oh, I cannot think how I said them!"

"After all," said Aulus, who had thought this out carefully, "you only said them in your fear of losing me. I should not hate you for that."

"And you do not hate me—do not hate me?" she half questioned, half asserted.

Aulus answered this as lovers may.

Presently he was puzzled at her long, fine-woven dress, her being here so near the villa in the morning.

"What is it?" he questioned. "Lævinus is here at the villa. What does it mean, you being here, too?"

Then she hurried to tell him of all her unexpected happiness. Aulus had to see a new Lævinus through her eyes, a glorified Lævinus he had never dreamed of.

"He is so kind, so beautiful and safe and kind," she said, her eyes shining. "He will never do anything to pain me. But, Aulus, you must help me. He said last night he wanted to marry me to Gnæus. Of course I would die first."

"Marry you to Gnæus! Well, that's the strangest yet. He hates Gnæus. He broke the betrothal with his daughter. Then they changed about, Father and he, and betrothed me to her. I had a terrible quarrel with my father because I refused. Then, after all, the poor little girl died."

"Poor little Lavinia!" said Chloé, loving for the first time this young sister who was gone from her.

She began to recall her father's words more exactly.

"I do not believe he said Gnæus—not the name Gnæus." She began to grow deeply excited. "He said only Cornelius's son. He said, 'my poor little Lavinia's betrothed.' Oh, do you suppose he meant you after all? You, Aulus!"

"Great gods in Olympus, of course he did!" cried Aulus, laughing aloud with happiness. "Oh, darling —they are on our side."

"Do you mean the gods are?" she inquired.

"No, the two fathers—both of them. They've fallen into a trap as though we had set it for them. Oh, dearest, dearest Chloé, so many difficulties, and now all—all are melted away."

He laughed again and whirled her about in a circle—a very dance of delight. The friends in Rome would not have recognized the sedate Aulus in this leaping, faunlike youth.

There was a sound in the garden.

"Father has come," said Chloé. "We must hurry and tell him."

"But that would never do. I'll come over this morning, a formal call, and consent with obedient grace to marry his daughter!" Aulus made a courtly bow, to show her how he would do it.

"What is the use of that?" she asked.

"Why, Chloé, he would be horrified that we are even acquainted before he has arranged it."

"Would he? But he loved my mother the same way."

"The formal call would be safer."

"Then perhaps I will not see you until evening. Perhaps not until tomorrow." Chloé's face was so doleful that Aulus laughed and consented to come into the garden.

But inside the garden they discovered that Lævinus

was not yet come. It was only Robina setting the table. She brought an extra chair for the guest. Romans at this time did not often recline at table.

A few moments later Lævinus, coming out into the bright sunshine, was surprised to see his daughter sitting at table side by side with a young man, the eyes of both demurely on their plates.

"What does this mean, Chloé?" he began.

Aulus sprang up.

"Please excuse us, sir. It was Chloé's idea to tell you—that—to tell you—well, how much we love each other." He was completely confused.

Chloé ran to Lævinus and caught his hand.

"Aulus said you would be angry. But you will not be angry. We have done no harm."

"Well, what have you done, anyway? How do you happen to be so friendly with a young man who last night seemed a monster to you?"

"I thought you meant Gnæus. Aulus is different. I will marry Aulus whenever you wish."

"Tut, tut, child—have you no manners at all?" said Lævinus. But he kissed her indulgently.

"Please do not be angry," reiterated Aulus. "You may not know that I was down here at the Villa Cornelia during my banishment. I met Chloé then and, sir, I knew she was your daughter. I always treated her as such."

"Well—since you are to be married, perhaps it is just as well that you love each other," consented Lævinus. "For it's very plain that you do. Chloé —so this was what you would not tell me last night."

"It was because we had quarreled, and Aulus was angry with me," she said.

"I was never angry with you," declared Aulus, and he thought it was true.

Lævinus was looking at the young man, so fresh-colored, so upstanding and honest, rather stocky as Romans were apt to be.

"Is it not a piece of good fortune," he remarked, "that I like you the best of any young man in Rome?"

ABOUT THE AUTHOR

Caroline Dale Snedeker was born in 1871 in New Harmony, Indiana. Her grandfather, Robert Owen, was a successful Scottish industrialist and social reformer who came to the United States and founded New Harmony in an effort to found an "ideal society." As a child in New Harmony, she saw Italian murals representing Greek gods and goddesses which fired her imagination and curiosity about ancient times and places.

Then, in 1903, she married Charles H. Snedeker, and, with his advice and encouragement, began to write. Her life-long interest in ancient times became a subject for careful study as Mrs. Snedeker read about history and traveled in Greece and Rome. The result was books such as THE FORGOTTEN DAUGHTER and THE WHITE ISLE.

When Caroline Dale Snedeker died in 1956, she left a legacy of books which continue to make the ancient world vivid and fascinating to readers.